"I don't want us to be frien

Angie continued with a wry quirk of her lips, "I want you too much for that to be possible."

Joshua's heart crashed against his rib cage with bruising force as blood rushed below his belt. "Where is this going?"

"Well, that depends." Her pink tongue flicked out and wet her lower lip. "Do you want me?"

"You know I want you."

"Do you plan on doing something about that?" A sultry smile spread across her face.

"It can only be sex." If he acted on this dangerous attraction, he had to make sure his feelings didn't get involved.

"Incredible, earth-shattering sex. So what's holding you back?"

He reached out and tucked a strand of hair behind her ear, and she shivered against his touch.

"What's holding me back from no-strings-attached sex?" He leaned in until their breaths mingled. "Nothing."

* * *

A Song of Secrets by Jayci Lee is part of the Hana Trio series.

Dear Reader,

Beginning this new series was incredibly exciting to me. Creating a brand-new world with a fresh cast of characters and exploring an entirely novel industry—all of it was a joy. But my favorite part was that I got to be immersed in music while I wrote *A Song of Secrets.*

I listened to a whole lot of Yo-Yo Ma and Jacqueline du Pré performances to prepare me to write the parts of our cellist heroine, Angie Han, and our composer hero, Joshua Shin. The beauty, nuance and passion of their relationship truly felt like music to me as their story flowed through my fingers.

I wrote this book smack in the middle of the pandemic and set it in a postpandemic world—dreaming of a postpandemic world. While the pandemic might have left its mark in some ways, my characters navigate the new normal with resilience and hope. And I believe that we all will when the time comes.

Thank you so much for choosing to read *A Song of Secrets.* I hope Angie and Joshua's story lifts your spirits and infuses you with joy.

With love,

Jayci Lee

JAYCI LEE

A SONG OF SECRETS

Recycling programs for this product may not exist in your area.

ISBN-13: 978-1-335-73542-3

A Song of Secrets

This is a work of fiction. Names, characters, places and incidents are either the product of the author's imagination or are used fictitiously. Any resemblance to actual persons, living or dead, businesses, companies, events or locales is entirely coincidental.

This edition published by arrangement with Harlequin Books S.A.

For questions and comments about the quality of this book, please contact us at CustomerService@Harlequin.com.

Harlequin Enterprises ULC
22 Adelaide St. West, 41st Floor
Toronto, Ontario M5H 4E3, Canada
www.Harlequin.com

Printed in U.S.A.

Jayci Lee writes poignant, sexy and laugh-out-loud romance every free second she can scavenge. She lives in sunny California with her tall, dark and handsome husband, two amazing boys with boundless energy and a fluffy rescue whose cuteness is a major distraction. At times, she cannot accommodate reality because her brain is full of drool-worthy heroes and badass heroines clamoring to come to life.

Because of all the books demanding to be written, Jayci writes full-time now and is semiretired from her fifteen-year career as a defense litigator. She loves food, wine and traveling, and, incidentally, so do her characters. Books have always helped her grow, dream and heal, and she hopes her books will do the same for you.

Books by Jayci Lee

Harlequin Desire

The Heirs of Hansol

Temporary Wife Temptation
Secret Crush Seduction
Off Limits Attraction

Hana Trio

A Song of Secrets

Visit her Author Profile page at Harlequin.com, or jaycilee.com, for more titles.

You can also find Jayci Lee on Facebook, along with other Harlequin Desire authors, at Facebook.com/harlequindesireauthors!

To my lovely father-in-law and mother-in-law.
Your support means the world to me.
Thank you.

Prologue

The Neimans' annual dinner was not Joshua Shin's usual scene. He was more accustomed to long hours in the office and longer hours sitting at his piano. But his grandfather wasn't feeling well and had asked him to attend in his place. He couldn't seem to deny his *halabuji* anything. He had hero-worshipped the man since he was able to tilt his head up.

So he'd acquiesced, knowing full well the dinner party was a fundraising event for the Chamber Music Society of Southern California—knowing that there was a chance *she* might be performing tonight. God, it was pathetic. After ten years, he still couldn't think about her without the familiar ache clenching his heart.

As he passed the wrought iron gates of the Beverly

Hills estate, a regal Georgian mansion came into view, gleaming with light against the dusk. Joshua maneuvered his Tesla to join the line of high-end cars in the driveway and entrusted his car to one of the valets in white jackets and black ties.

A flute of champagne was thrust into his hand as he walked through the front door. Newly arrived guests mingled in the circular grand foyer before moving on to the ballroom. But the thread of anxiety running through him made Joshua rather antisocial. He nodded politely to the other guests and proceeded into the ballroom, claiming a spot near the rich emerald drapes of one of the floor-to-ceiling windows.

He couldn't stop his eyes from sweeping across the room, searching for a face he dreamed of too often. To his…relief, she was nowhere in sight. It was unlikely that out of close to a hundred musicians with the Chamber Music Society, Angie Han would be one of the performers. Then again, the musicians would've been herded in through the service entrance and relegated to the back rooms, so he wouldn't see her until the performance even if she were here.

Irritation licked at him at the thought of her being treated like a second-class citizen, but he stopped himself short. What the hell business was it of his how she was treated? She'd been out of his life for a decade, and he wanted to keep it that way.

"Mr. Shin," a cool, cultured voice said from behind him.

"Yes?" Joshua turned to find a silver-haired man in an impeccable suit regarding him.

"I'm Timothy Pearce, the executive director of the Chamber Music Society," he said. "I'm surprised not to see your grandfather here tonight. He rather enjoys these small, intimate performances."

"He regrets missing it and sent me in his stead." Joshua didn't volunteer the reason for his grandfather's absence.

"Well, you are very welcome here." He assessed Joshua with calculating eyes before a charming smile spread across his face. The man was obviously gauging whether he'd be as generous a donor as his grandfather. "We're always thrilled to see the younger generation join in the appreciation of classical music."

"I do share my grandfather's love of music." Joshua saw no harm in reassuring him. He had every intention of donating as his grandfather would have. "Speaking of which, what do you have lined up for tonight's performance?"

"You're in for a treat." Timothy Pearce's smile had warmed by ten degrees with Joshua's reassurance. "The Hana Trio will be playing for us."

He exerted every ounce of his self-control to keep the shock from showing on his face. Angie was the cellist in the ensemble, with her two sisters on the violin and the viola. While he'd been aware of the possibility, the thought of actually seeing her tonight sent his mind spiraling.

"You *have* heard of them, right?" The other man cocked his head to the side when the silence stretched on a moment too long. "They are a phenomenal up-and-coming string trio."

"Yes, of course," he said through numb lips, feigning polite interest. "I'm looking forward to their performance."

"Wonderful. It was a pleasure meeting you, and I hope you enjoy the rest of the evening." The executive director walked off to greet to a jovial older couple just entering the ballroom.

What Joshua said about his love of music was true, but it went much deeper than that. There was once a time when music was his life. Images of sunlight streaming down on his fingers as they flew over the piano and sounds of beautiful music and laughter flitted through his mind. Happiness, sweet and full of hope, filled his soul before reality slashed through it, leaving it in pitiful tatters. She had ruined it all.

Deep in his thoughts, Joshua belatedly noticed the guests migrating out of the ballroom. He followed the herd to an impressive conservatory opening up to a manicured garden, its vastness obscured by the coming night. The string lights on the glass ceiling sparkled against the darkening sky, and the elegant lamps around the room added to the beauty and intimacy of the space.

When the throng of people in front of him dispersed to take their seats, the makeshift stage at the far end of the room came into view. That was when he saw her. *Angie*. Everything else melted away and the only sound he could hear was the drumming of his heart.

In the years they'd been apart, she'd gone from a lovely girl to a breathtaking woman. The black silky hair she used to pull into careless ponytails lay shimmering on her shoulders. The slight slimming of her face highlighted her cheekbones and added an alluring sharpness to her soft features. He couldn't tear his gaze away from her. Fortunately, her eyes were downcast, her slender arms and long, graceful fingers poised over the cello as she tuned her instrument with her sisters.

Before she could glance up and see him, Joshua situated himself by the doorsill, concealed by a tall, leafy plant. Some of the stragglers passing by glanced curiously at him, but they soon took their seats. A hush fell across the room and the concert began.

The first strains of the music sent a shiver through his body and raised goose bumps on his arms. Angie had been a talented and promising musician in college, but her sound had matured into something nuanced and silken that caressed his senses. He'd listened to the Hana Trio's debut album while visiting his grandfather, so he knew they played beautifully…but hearing them live was something else entirely. True to their name—*hana* meant *one* in Korean—they played as a united whole, and the result was exquisite.

He closed his eyes and let the music wash over him, smoothing out the jagged edges of his rampaging emotions. He felt nothing for Angie Han. Not even anger. The fury, pain, and…yearning that filled him were mere echoes from his past. It hadn't been easy but he'd moved on from her long ago. This sentimentality wasn't like him.

It was a fine performance and Joshua clapped

along with the resounding applause of the audience. He hated the nervous trip of his heartbeat, wondering what he would do when she saw him. Staying partially hidden behind the plant, he watched as the trio stood and took their bows. He was being ridiculous. She was a musician and he was there as a patron of the Chamber Music Society. If she saw him, he would greet her politely like an old acquaintance and go on with his life. With an irritated huff, he stepped away from the doorsill and joined the rest of the guests in the conservatory.

"Ladies and gentlemen." Timothy Pearce raised his voice to be heard over the excited chatter, and Joshua dutifully gave him his attention. "I want to thank the wonderful Mr. and Mrs. Neiman for hosting this amazing dinner. And I sincerely thank each and every one of you for joining us. You can continue to enjoy and foster beautiful chamber music like tonight's Hana Trio performance by making a generous donation to the Chamber Music Society."

Joshua's sense of someone watching him grew as the executive director continued his smooth fundraising pitch. The pinprick of awareness started at his head and spread all the way down his spine. Slowly, he turned his head to find Angie's wide, horrified eyes on him. She had paled until no hint of color remained on her cheeks, and her mouth was open slightly as though a gasp had just escaped from it.

As their eyes met and held, Joshua couldn't breathe. His body heated up and his hands flexed by his sides as though remembering the feel of her. *No.* He refused to give her even a sliver of his emotions. He held her gaze for a split second longer and gave the barest nod of his head to acknowledge her. Then he looked away from her and faced Pearce again in time to hear the end of his speech.

"You are part of our family. Thank you."

The hearty applause faded and conversation filled the room. Unconsciously, Joshua's eyes sought her out once more, only to glimpse the back of her as she left the conservatory through the door leading out to the garden. Disappointment flitted through him before being replaced by irritation. He didn't regret not speaking to her. There was nothing left to say between them other than forced pleasantries that he had no patience for.

As the rest of the guests headed to the dining room for dinner, Joshua stopped Timothy Pearce to hand him a check. He'd come to the party and stayed for the performance. His grandfather wouldn't mind if he didn't sit through a stuffy meal with a roomful of strangers. When he'd said his goodbyes to the executive director, he made his way across the deserted grand foyer to the door.

"Joshua," a quiet voice said from the corridor.

He spun at the sound of his name. Angie took hesitant steps into the foyer but stopped long before she reached him.

"What do you want?" He grimaced at the simmering anger in his tone—a telltale sign that he wasn't immune to her.

"I… I just wanted to say hello." She wrung her hands before dropping them to her sides and curling them into fists. "I wanted to know that you're… happy."

"Happy?" His bark of laughter tasted as bitter as crushed aspirins in his throat. "You don't expect me to dignify that with a response, do you?"

"I'm so sorry, Joshua," she said, her voice catching on his name.

Something snapped inside him and he stormed across the room until he loomed over her. She was suddenly so close that he could feel the heat coming off her body. The shock of her proximity paralyzed him and all he could do was stare down at her upturned face. Neither of them moved a muscle as awareness swirled around them and their breathing quickened. The tension grew unbearably taut as the seconds ticked by. Faint laughter in the distance ripped him out of his trance.

"You don't get to know if I'm *happy*. You don't get to say you're sorry," he said in a low growl, reining in the desire pounding through his veins. "You forfeited that right when you left me ten years ago."

A vise threatened to crush his heart when a single tear rolled down her cheek, and he hated her for it. He hated her for making him want to wipe away the tear and gather her into his arms. For making him wish for things he could never have again. For making him want *her* again—even for a passing second.

He turned on his heel and walked out of the mansion without a backward glance. She threatened the equilibrium he'd worked so hard to achieve. Never again. Angie Han meant nothing to him anymore.

One

Two months later

After rehearsing with her sisters, Angie hurried to the parking lot of the community college where they rented a classroom for their practices. She had a meeting with Janet Miller, her mentor and the Chamber Music Society's artistic director.

She unlocked her car and opened the rear door—her semicompact didn't have enough trunk space for her cello—while humming a song under her breath. The melody had been stuck in her head for weeks but she hadn't been able to place it. Maybe it was something her mom used to sing for her when she was little. It was such a lovely tune. Once she finagled her instrument into the back seat, angled just right so she could still see through the rear window, she slipped into the driver's seat and steered her car out of the parking spot.

Anxiety ran through her as her thoughts turned to her meeting with Janet. The Chamber Music Society was struggling to remain afloat after the pandemic. All concerts, fundraising events and in-home performances for their highest donors had ceased with the lockdown, which meant much of their funding had also come to a halt. If it hadn't been for their most dedicated benefactors, the many musicians of the society would've already been without a home. With the new season only a few months away, she was hoping things would eventually return to normal—whatever that meant these days. But the situation could be more dire than she'd thought.

She had her radio set to her favorite classical music station and smiled as Erik Satie's Gymnopédie no. 1 came through the speakers. The French composer's music was her catnip. For some reason, it always made her imagine the world moving in that peculiar way it did in silent movies. The piece infused her with much-needed serenity as she arrived at her friend's office and knocked lightly on the open door.

"My dear, it's so lovely to see you," Janet said, embracing her warmly.

"It's good to see you, too." Angie hugged her back tightly.

There had been times she'd wanted to quit music, believing herself to lack the talent to *make* it. But her mentor had always been there to remind her that she had the talent, passion and drive to succeed as a musician. She wouldn't be where she was without Janet.

"Why don't we sit by the window?" Her friend led her to the cozy seating area and they sat side by side on the plush love seat. "Do you want something to drink?"

"No, thanks. I'm fine," Angie said with a hint of impatience. Her heart picked up pace, anxious to find out what this meeting was about. "Tell me what's going on."

Even before she answered, Janet's resigned sigh confirmed her worst fears. "The Chamber Music Society's financial situation is even grimmer than we'd initially thought. The success of this coming season is crucial to its survival. The board intimated at the last meeting that if we don't pull off the best season we've ever had, it might be the end of the society."

"Just like that?" she whispered.

"Just like that." Her friend looked down at her hands.

Janet's hesitation told Angie there was more to the bad news. "And?"

Reluctance in every line of her face, her mentor said, "And Timothy wants you and your sisters to ask your father for help."

"But…he stopped supporting the society when I cut ties with him," she stuttered, rattled by the request.

"I know. I hate asking this of you, but I also understand where Timothy is coming from. Really, every donation will increase the chance of our survival. And your father used to be one of our top donors."

Angie looked out the window at the streets and buildings baking in the Los Angeles sun. "Let me think about it."

She couldn't refuse her mentor outright no matter how much she wanted to. And the fate of the Chamber Music Society wasn't just about her. Her sisters and all the other musicians would suffer right along with her.

"That's all I can ask for." Janet reached out and gently grasped her hand. "Thank you."

"Of course. I want to do my part in saving the society." She pulled her hand out of Janet's after a quick squeeze. "I'll let you get back to work."

She walked to the parking lot with heavy steps. Her father would never support the society because it was the source of Angie's livelihood—her independence. Even though her sisters had a better relationship with him, he wouldn't budge for them either if it meant helping her, too.

Still, she had to try, didn't she?

Once she got in her car, she pulled out her cellphone from her purse and dialed her father's number before she lost her nerve. He picked up after the fourth ring.

"Let me guess," her father drawled. "You want something from me."

Her hand clenched around her phone as anger and humiliation assailed her. Setting aside her pride, she said, "The Chamber Music Society needs your help."

"And why would I help them?" He sounded almost bored.

"Umma supported them when she was alive," she said quietly.

There was a long pause, then he said in a tired voice, "Come home, Angie. I'll donate to them if you cease your childish rebellion and come back home."

Her throat tightened with emotion—it had been five years since she'd spoken to her father—but leaving home had not been a childish rebellion. She refused to give him the leverage to control her life again.

"That's not my home anymore." She blinked away the tears that threatened to fall. "I'll find another way to help the society. Goodbye, Appa."

She headed home with a heavy heart. Home was a small one-bedroom apartment on the outskirts of downtown Los Angeles. Outdated and located in a not-quite-rough neighborhood, it meant more to her than a mansion could. It was her first real place that wasn't her father's house.

Her mom had fought cancer for five long years, and Angie was glad she'd been at her side. But once her mother was gone, she couldn't stand living with her demanding father and the constant reminder of what he'd made her do. Even his threat to cut her off completely wasn't enough to stop her from branching out on her own. She didn't want his damn money. Not then and not now.

She maneuvered her car into her narrow parking space, then waited listlessly for the creaky elevator to take her to the lobby. After checking her mailbox, she took another cramped ride upstairs and walked down what felt like miles of dimly lit hallway. When she finally arrived at her apartment, she shuffled inside, limp with sudden exhaustion. Even so, she carefully stowed away her cello in her practice corner before she collapsed onto the couch, kicking off the sensible pumps she'd worn into the living room.

"Home." She smiled against a soft cushion.

The old, dated building was what it was, but she had made her apartment as warm and cozy as she could with her limited budget. She might have overdone it a bit with the table lamps and floor lamps, but she loved how brightly lit her place was. With bursts of color from the pillows and throws, and a collection of whimsical posters splashed across the walls, it was home sweet home.

But her smile soon faded. The quiet peace of her meticulously constructed life had been disrupted by the uncertain future of the Chamber Music Society...and a ghost from her past. What happened at the Neimans' dinner invaded her thoughts without warning, and Angie scrunched her eyes shut against the memory of Joshua's fury. Even after two months, her heart still ached at the confirmation of her worst fears. Joshua Shin hated her.

She'd convinced herself that she'd moved past it. That she'd forgotten how she'd broken his heart and her own by leaving him. But seeing him after all these years broke the dam that had held everything in check. Holding back her emotions had been the only way she was able to continue her life without him. But now...

No, what she felt was regret at what could've been. Nothing more. She couldn't still want him. He hated her. There could never be anything between them. She'd blown that chance ten years ago. She impatiently wiped away the tears on her cheeks and took a shaky breath. She had no time to dwell on the past when the present urgently required her attention.

Her father would only help the Chamber Music Society if Angie agreed to his condition, but she couldn't throw away her hard-earned independence. Besides, his donation alone wouldn't be enough to save the society. What was she going to do? With a heaving sigh, she sat up and said, "Alexa, play KUSC."

She needed the company of classical music tonight. And a nice cup of tea. After a brief trip to the kitchen, she settled back on the sofa with a steaming mug, and embraced the tranquility the music so generously offered her.

A new piece by the composer known only as A.S. filled her living room. He'd burst onto the classical music scene a few years ago, and the mastery of his work and the mystery of his identity made him an overnight phenomenon. Angie tended to like what she heard when his music came on the radio.

In the next moment, the small, appreciative smile on her face cracked and slipped.

"No, it can't be," she whispered, her fingers fluttering to her lips. The part in the piece had already passed, but she was certain it was the melody she'd been humming incessantly for the last couple months. But how could that be if this was the first time she was hearing the composition?

She quickly downloaded the piece onto her best-of

playlist and frantically fast-forwarded to the part that had jarred her memories awake. She rewound to the same spot and replayed it. Again and again. A shaky sigh shivered past her lips.

Maybe it had to do with seeing Joshua again after all these years. Maybe it had to do with her long forgotten memories flooding her mind. But something had awakened the tune inside her, and she could finally place where it was from. It was his. It was the melody he'd played for her in college, shyly telling her he was working on a cello concerto for her. It was *her* melody.

She'd discovered a secret that irrevocably entwined her with Joshua. Because the same melody he'd played for her back then was coming through her speakers right this minute. He was the genius behind the anonymous pieces. He was A.S.

And now I know.

Angie bolted to her feet. Blood pounded in her ears and her breath came in shallow pants. She knew how to save the Chamber Music Society. And Joshua Shin was going to hate her for it. But what of it? He couldn't hate her any more than he already did.

Joshua spun in his chair and stared out the window, barely registering the sprawling view of downtown Los Angeles from his forty-eighth-floor office. With an exasperated sigh, he shoved his hands through his already tousled hair.

Dozens of reports and proposals awaited his approval, but his concentration was shot. He hadn't slept properly in two months, and last night was no different. He'd drifted from one dream to the next—or maybe they'd been memories. He couldn't pin down whether he'd been remembering or dreaming but he was certain that Angie Han had been the focus.

Just one moment with her—it couldn't have been more than five minutes—and he couldn't erase her from his thoughts. *Goddammit.* How could he allow her to have such control over him after all these years? He couldn't. He wouldn't. She'd already taken too much from him. He'd spent six years of his life not composing music because of her. He'd lost an essential part of himself because it had hurt too much. She wasn't taking another second of his time.

He swiveled back to face his desk, and returned to the report he'd been reviewing. Through sheer bullheadedness, he reviewed four more reports and a proposal before Angie invaded his thoughts again. God, she played so beautifully. He'd once dreamed of writing her a cello concerto, so she could perform his music for the world to hear. *That's enough.* He wasn't a heartsick twenty-year-old anymore.

He was the vice president of operations of Riddle Incorporated, an electronic components company started by his grandfather. He was slated to become its new CEO in a few months. The livelihood of over nine hundred employees rested on his shoulders. There was no time to waste daydreaming about an old flame. And that was all she was. She didn't define who he was.

He turned his attention back to his job and succeeded in keeping it there. His focus only broke when his phone rang. Mildly irritated by the interruption, he hit the speaker button. "Yes, Janice?"

"Sorry to disturb you, but there is a Ms. Angie Han here to see you," his executive assistant said. "I asked her to make an appointment and return another time, but she insists on waiting. She said you two went to college together."

Disbelief filled Joshua. It wasn't enough she'd occupied his thoughts and dreams for the past two months. She had to show up in person. Should he send her away? He didn't owe her anything. He didn't have to see her. But could he stand not knowing why she'd come? *Hell.*

"Please send her in."

He steepled his fingers and kept his gaze on the door. There wasn't anything he could do about the thundering of his heart, but he was determined to greet her with utter indifference.

She walked through the door, her chin held high. With her back ramrod straight and shoulders pulled back, she looked ready for battle. When her eyes met his, they flitted away, but only for a second. She quickly turned her determined gaze back to him and strode up to his desk.

He waved a casual hand at one of his guest chairs, and she sat without a word. He tried and failed to ignore how beautiful she looked in her slim black pants and soft, barely pink blouse. She was close enough that he could smell her sweet vanilla perfume—the same scent she wore a decade ago. His body remembered only too well, and a tremor ran through him. Had she worn it to get to him? And why would she want to get to him? His mind spun and he grappled for equilibrium.

"Hello, Joshua." Her smooth, melodic voice felt like a warm caress.

His lips went numb and refused to form her name, so he demanded, "What are you doing here?"

"After the Neimans' dinner..." She didn't need to go on for him to remember their heated encounter at the party. The same rush of lust and anger stirred in him now. "I knew you wouldn't agree to see me if I tried to make an appointment."

"You haven't answered my question," he said with a hard edge in his voice.

Her eyes fell to her hands—again only for the briefest second—then met his. "I have a proposal for you."

"What could you possibly propose to me? You made it clear you wanted nothing to do with me when you left to protect your precious trust fund." He bit his tongue, and stopped the bitter words spewing from his mouth. These feelings should've faded into an unpleasant memory he could shrug away by now.

"I can't change what happened between us. I wish I could explain..." she said in a near whisper. "But I assure you this proposal is purely business."

"Get out." A drop of sweat slid down his neck. He hated that his body still craved her after all this time when he wanted nothing to do with her.

And what business could she have with him? Was she here on her father's behalf? Their companies had been rivals for decades. That was why her father had threatened to disown her when he found out they were together. Even though recent changes in Riddle's business direction finally ended that rivalry, Joshua couldn't imagine the two companies ever collaborating on anything.

When she made no move to leave, he turned his chair to face the windows, underscoring her dismissal.

"I know who you are." Her voice was so soft, he probably misheard her. Still, his stomach dropped like a stone to his feet.

He slowly faced her again and enunciated with care, "What did you say?"

"I know. I know you're A.S."

"Who the hell is A.S.?" he scoffed, panic slapping awake his befuddled brain. It couldn't be. No one knew. Not even his grandfather. He had to tread cautiously. "I don't know what game you're playing at, but I believe I asked you to leave."

The last thing he expected was for her to sing. But sing she did. She hummed the theme of his latest piece, and like a breeze blowing through the window, his memory returned to him with startling clarity. How could he have forgotten?

It was her melody. The first sapling of the concerto he'd dreamt of writing for her. But that dream had died with his heartbreak. Or so he'd thought. Somehow, it had resurfaced as one of the themes of his latest piece. How could he not have recognized it? Because it was no longer hers. The melody was just a part of one of his works. It had nothing to do with her.

"That's enough," he snapped.

Angie clamped her mouth shut at his rough tone, but there was a triumphant light in her eyes. "You *are* A.S."

He wasn't about to tell a bold-faced lie when they both knew she had him. "And what do you plan to do with that juicy tidbit?"

"Please. Don't take offense." She bit her bottom lip and bright blotches of pink stained her cheeks. Inexplicable satisfaction filled him as he watched her placid demeanor crack. "I just need your help."

"If you're here to blackmail me, at least own up to it," he drawled, cold cynicism hardening his features. "Do you expect me to provide you with something in exchange for your silence?"

"I don't even understand why my silence is worth something to you in the first place," she said, her voice unsteady. "Why do you need to compose in secret?"

Despite his feigned nonchalance, he couldn't breathe properly. At first, he'd kept his identity a secret to avoid conflict with his father, who had never approved of his pursuit of music. But now, his family's legacy was at stake.

If the board of directors found out Joshua was a composer *on the side*, it could affect their decision to appoint him as the next CEO. His competition, Nathan Whitley, would have a field day waving it around as proof that Joshua wasn't as dedicated to Riddle as he was. His grandfather and father would be devastated if the career CEO beat him out on the position.

"That isn't exactly the kind of information I would

share with my blackmailer, now, is it?" He leaned back in his chair and let disdain stain his words. "Are you trying to gather more ammunition to use against me?"

"I'm not going to reveal your secret," she said with quiet determination. "But I still need your help."

"And I have no reason to help you without that leverage." He bared his teeth in a jagged imitation of a smile.

"The Chamber Music Society is facing a financial crisis, and this upcoming season can make or break us," she continued doggedly. Her tenacity used to impress him, but now it only frustrated him. He needed her to leave. "I would like to commission A.S. on behalf of the society to compose a new piece for us to premiere on opening night. It'll give us the boost we need to propel the season forward and draw the attention we need."

"You have no intention of revealing to the world that I'm A.S.?"

"No. None whatsoever." She met his gaze and held it, and he believed her. She'd always been honest to a fault. He was fortunate she was unchanged in that regard.

"Then my answer to your proposition is no." He hardened himself against her crestfallen expression. If his secret was safe, then he didn't want to risk having more interactions with her. She was no longer a threat to his heart, but he desired her with an intensity that he didn't want to test. Her presence in his office alone shook him to the core. Spending more time with her was out of the question. "But I'm not without sympathy for the Chamber Music Society's situation. I can make another donation..."

"I don't want your money," she cut him off sharply then clamped her mouth shut. After a deep breath, she continued in an even tone, "The money will only get us so far. But a collaboration between A.S. and the Chamber Music Society will create the kind of buzz we need to make the upcoming season a success. It'll increase ticket sales and garner new donors." She sat forward in the chair. "It'll breathe new life into the society."

"My answer is still no," he said, ignoring the stab of guilt. He wasn't about to apologize for his decision when she was in no position to ask favors of him.

Angie stood from her seat with quiet composure, and he got to his feet with her. She opened her small purse and drew a simple, elegant business card from it. "That's my cellphone number. Please call me if you change your mind."

He took the card from her and said with finality, "I won't."

She left his office just as she'd come in, back straight and head held high, leaving lingering notes of vanilla in her wake. He'd done the right thing. Getting himself entangled with Angie Han spelled disaster for his sanity. Then why did he feel like such a bastard?

Joshua spent the rest of the day putting Angie out of his mind. The Neimans' party and her visit today were minor glitches. She was out of his life and it was going to stay that way. Then why couldn't he slow down his heart? It was merely a physical reaction to an unexpected occurrence. He would forget all about her by tomorrow.

A part of him wanted to admit defeat and acknowledge that he was worthless at work while his mind was spinning and coming to terms with Angie's visit. But the more stubborn side of him insisted that he could still get more work done, so he stayed at his desk, staring unseeingly at the computer screen until the sun dipped below the horizon.

When his cell phone rang, he was relieved at the interruption. "Hello, Mother."

"Hello, son." She failed miserably at sounding chipper.

"What's wrong?" He straightened in his seat.

"Can't a mother call her son just because?" There was a slight tremor to her voice. Now he was really worried.

"Can't a mother just tell her son the truth without worrying him to death?" he said with a touch of irritation, and was immediately contrite. "Sorry, Mom. Tell me what's going on."

"Don't be too alarmed. It was a minor one and he's stable now but… Halabuji had a heart attack." A sob broke free from his mother. "He's been admitted to the Cedars-Sinai Medical Center. Let's talk when you get here."

Joshua's heart stuttered with fear. "I'm leaving now."

Two

Angie sat soaking in a much-needed bath, her knees drawn above the bubbles to fit into the cramped tub. She trailed her hand up her wet arm, remembering the surreal day she'd had. Had she really barged into Joshua's office, thinking she could blackmail him into helping the Chamber Music Society?

It hadn't taken her long to realize that she didn't have it in her to blackmail someone. Especially the man she had once loved. She'd sworn to herself that she would do anything to help save the Chamber Music Society, but as she sat across from Joshua, his handsome face taut with worry, she couldn't bring herself to do it.

Instead, she had wanted to wrap herself around him and kiss away his worries. Angie sank down into the tub, immersing her head underwater. She must've been out of her mind. But she couldn't help but wonder why it was so important for him to keep his identity as A.S. a secret.

Suddenly feeling restless, she finished washing up and stepped out of the bath. Just as she wrapped a towel around herself, she heard her cell phone ringing. Her heart slammed against her rib cage. It could be anyone. One of her sisters probably. Then why was she running to her room at breakneck speed?

When she grabbed her phone from the nightstand, she saw that it was indeed her sister. She wished she could unfeel the disappointment that shot through her. "Hey, Meg. What's up?"

"I have a brilliant idea to save the Chamber Music Society," Megan said without preamble.

"What is it?" Angie asked, hope sparking to life.

"We need to get everyone together and do one of those calendars. You know, like the ones firefighters do?"

Her hope fizzled out like a wet candle. "How can you joke about this?"

"No, hear me out. We'll call it the 'Hotties of Chamber Music,'" her sister prattled, "and have our finest pose for the photos."

"Like Arthur, our principal cellist?" Angie randomly named one of her colleagues.

"Totally. He's pretty hot for a man in his sixties, but I'm not sure he'd take his shirt off for the photo shoot."

There was only one reason for this silliness. "How many bags of Sour Patch Kids have you eaten today?"

"Three."

"Full size?"

"Yes." She could practically hear Megan twitching from the sugar high. "What of it?"

"Go eat some real food, and call me when you have a helpful idea." She shivered when a drop of water from her hair rolled down her back.

"Can't we chat for a bit? I'm bored."

"And I'm freezing. I just got out of the bath. I need to put some clothes on." Angie walked to her dresser and pulled out her favorite leggings and a hoodie. "Don't forget. Real food. Bye."

As she poked her head out of her hoodie, her cell rang again. Wrangling her arm through the hole, she answered the call. "We are not shooting the 'Hotties of Chamber Music.'"

There was silence on the other end, and mortification spread through her. She didn't need to look at the screen to know that the caller wasn't Megan. *It's okay.* It would be fine as long as it wasn't Joshua.

"Why not?" a deep, amused voice drawled. "That just might give the Chamber Music Society the boost it needs."

Maybe it was someone else with the same sexy voice as her ex.

"This is Joshua, by the way."

Shit. She scrunched her eyes shut, wishing the floor would suck her in like quicksand. Why the hell was he calling her anyway?

"Joshua? What a surprise," she said stiffly, while pushing her other arm through the hoodie.

"You did give me your phone number," he reminded her.

"And you said you won't be calling me," she countered.

"I changed my mind." The cool arrogance of his tone—as though he had every right to do whatever the hell he wanted—was maddening.

A sharp retort formed on the tip of her tongue, but she clamped her mouth shut. He'd changed his mind? Did that mean he'd changed his mind about calling her? Or changed his mind about her proposal? She sat down on the corner of her bed and forced herself to release the breath she'd been holding.

"Changed your mind how?" she asked.

"I'm willing to consider your proposal…for a price."

"Of…of course. The Chamber Music Society will pay you for the commissioned work…"

"I don't want to take money from a struggling organization," he dismissed. "That's not what I want."

"Then what is it that you want?" Her hands shook with anticipation. "What's your price?"

"It's… I need…" He sighed deeply. "Is there any way we can meet?"

"Right now?" She glanced at the clock; it was close to ten.

"Yes, now."

"Um…where?" The thought of seeing him again made her heart race.

"Wherever is convenient for you. It won't take long," he said curtly, reminding her that this was purely business.

"There's a coffee shop down the street..."

"I'll meet you there. What's it called?"

She told him the name of the café and hung up. They were meeting in half an hour. She loathed to change out of her comfortable sweats and considered showing up wearing them. But this was a business meeting. She wasn't meeting a friend for coffee.

As she blow-dried her long, damp hair, she tamped down the excitement bubbling up inside her. She was about to meet a man who hated her to find out what he wanted from her in exchange for helping the Chamber Music Society. What was there to be excited about?

She put on a pair of slim black pants and a light gray sweater. She didn't have it in her to put on any makeup, so she smeared on some tinted lip balm and pronounced herself presentable.

The café was only two blocks away, and she arrived a few minutes early. She ordered a chamomile tea, and found a table by the window facing the street.

How many times had they met in cozy cafés like this to work on their homework or study for an exam? A wistful smile curled her lips as she remembered the warmth and simplicity of those days. She wished she hadn't taken them for granted. But she'd had no idea their days were numbered. They were supposed to have a lifetime together.

Angie pushed away her crushing pain, startled by its intensity. Over the past ten years, it had ebbed into a dull ache in the back of her heart. Seeing Joshua made the old scars gape and bleed. She didn't understand. Did she still have feelings for him after all this time? That would be foolish. She was confusing nostalgia with reawakened emotions.

Taking a sip of her tea, she stared unseeingly at the dark street outside. They weren't carefree kids in love anymore. Tonight, they were meeting under very different circumstances, so she needed to have her head on straight.

"Did I keep you waiting?" Joshua asked, pulling out the chair across from her.

"Oh." The moment she heard his voice, her heart rattled as though a jack-in-the-box had popped open. Heat rushed through her as she registered his disheveled hair and rolled-up sleeves, revealing strong forearms. His tie and jacket from earlier in the day were gone, and the sight of his chest and biceps filling out his shirt made her mind go blank. So much for straight thinking. "No, not at all. I just got here, too."

"Good." He ran his fingers through his hair, making it stick out all over the place.

Angie liked him better this way. The cold, immaculate man she'd met in his office was a stranger, but she saw hints of the old Joshua in this version. Someone who wouldn't completely shut her out. Maybe they would be able to work something out to help the Chamber Music Society after all.

"Do you want to order a drink before we get started?" Once she forced herself to stop ogling his body, she noticed the tension in the corners of his eyes and the weary downward turn of his mouth. Something was wrong.

"No, it's late." He pinched the bridge of his nose. "I don't want to take up too much of your time."

"So what is this *price* you require?" She wanted to find out what was going on with him. Her gut told her it had everything to do with his sudden about-face.

"My grandfather had a heart attack." His nostrils flared subtly as he took a deep breath. Joshua was hiding it well, but she saw it. He was hurting, and she couldn't do anything about the distress burrowing into her. She fought to keep her expression politely sympathetic, and nodded for him to continue. "I want you to play for him while he recuperates."

Whatever she'd expected, it certainly wasn't that. "You want me to play for him?"

"His doctor believes music therapy will be invaluable to his recovery, and you're the obvious choice for a number of reasons," he said with frustration stamped across his features. While he might believe her to be the logical choice, he wasn't happy about it. "My grandfather is a devoted fan of the Hana Trio, and the cello is my grandfather's favorite instrument."

"If you're looking for a music therapist, I'm sure I could find you some highly recommended ones..."

"Is it below you to play for one old man?" he said scathingly.

"What?" She lowered her voice when a couple of heads turned their way. "It's because I don't think I'm qualified. Music therapy entails more than just playing music, and you could find someone better suited than me."

"I doubt there are many concert-level cellists providing music therapy. My grandfather has a discerning ear, and listening to an amateur play will have the opposite of a restorative effect on him." He sighed harshly. "And there's something about your sound. There's depth and heart to it that can touch people. It's…special."

Her mouth opened and closed several times. "Thank you, but…"

"I want you," he growled. Heat pooled in her stomach even though she knew what he meant. "I don't want a substitute. I want *you* to play for my grandfather. That's the deal."

"You forgot to add, *Take it or leave it,*" she said wryly.

A ghost of a smile came and went. "If you agree to play for my grandfather, I'll compose a new piece for the Hana Trio to premiere during the Chamber Music Society's upcoming season."

What could she say? She still had reservations about her effectiveness as a music therapist, but she would be happy to help his grandfather in any way. And she would be giving the Chamber Music Society a real chance to thrive.

"I remember how close you were to your grandfather," she murmured, gathering her thoughts.

"I still am." He leaned forward on the small table, bringing them closer together. "I can't *not* ask this of you, knowing it's what my grandfather needs. I would do anything for him."

Joshua hadn't wanted anything to do with her the last two times they'd met. From his tense posture and the wariness in his eyes, she could tell that hadn't changed. He just loved his grandfather enough to sacrifice what he wanted and, God help her, that moved her more than anything.

She cleared her throat. "How often would you need me to play for him?"

"I'll need to check with his doctor to see what would be most effective, but twice a week makes sense for now."

"Will you be with your grandfather when I play for him?" She didn't want to interact with him more than necessary. Getting over him had been one of the hardest things she'd ever done.

"I'll be there the first day to introduce you to him, but it's unlikely I'll be there after that."

She nodded, refusing to acknowledge the disappointment that pierced her at his response.

"Do we have a deal?" He studied her face intently as he waited for her answer.

"We have a deal."

Joshua arrived at the hospital earlier than their meeting time, not wanting Angie to lug around her hefty instrument in search of him. He planted himself close to the main entrance so he would be hard to miss.

After they parted last night, he repeatedly questioned his decision to bring Angie into his family's plight. His grandfather's sudden heart attack had sent a shock wave through Joshua and his parents. They were prepared to do anything to prevent it from happening again. When the doctor recommended music therapy as part of his grandfather's treatment, he immediately thought of Angie.

The cello was Halabuji's favorite instrument and he was especially enthralled by Angie's playing. That had to be the reason why Joshua had thought of her… That and the fact that he hadn't been able to stop thinking about her for the last two months. He cursed under his breath. He refused to believe that he'd brought her into this just so he could have her in his orbit. That was the last thing he wanted.

What he'd said about her sound being special was true. It had been true when they were together, and she had only improved with time. Listening to her play would help lower Halabuji's stress level and stabilize his condition. More importantly, it would make his grandfather happy. That was what mattered most.

Joshua hadn't asked Angie to play so he could have her back in his life. He'd asked her *despite* the fact he didn't want her in his life because it was the best thing he could do for his grandfather. That had to be it.

But for this to work, he had to control his unwanted attraction to her. As worried as he was last night, his body had trembled with lust at the sight of her. Her face had been scrubbed clean of makeup and she reminded him so much of her younger self. The one who had been his. He would've kissed that Angie deeply before he sat down across from her. They would've held hands across the table, her warmth giving him solace. And he would've taken her home and made love to her, soaking up the comfort she offered. He no longer wanted any of that, but his body insisted on craving her nonetheless.

"Joshua," Angie said, standing in front of him. Lost in his thoughts, he hadn't seen her come into the lobby.

"Thank you for coming." His voice was huskier than he would've liked. Her form-hugging jeans and light beige sweater emphasized her soft curves, which did nothing to curb his libido. *Goddammit.* He had to get a grip.

"Of course," she said in an all-business tone. If she'd noticed his hungry eyes lingering on her, she was doing a great job not showing it. "Should we go see him?"

He nodded curtly and led them to the set of elevators that would take them to the private rooms. His grandfather's room was almost at the end of the corridor so he wouldn't be disturbed by the elevator or the central hub of the nurses' station. They didn't say a word to each other as they made their way there.

Joshua stole a glance at Angie, who was dragging the tall, wide cello case beside her. He hadn't even offered to help; he'd been too busy lusting after her. Feeling like a jerk, he cleared his throat and asked, "Do you need help with your instrument?"

"Oh, please. I used to lug this baby from one end of the campus to the other. This is nothing." Her smile quickly faded as though she'd realized what she'd just said.

"I remember," he said casually.

He remembered all too well. He used to fuss about it back then, too. But they were in no position to reminisce about the old times. Even as the bitterness rolled in, Joshua kept his lips from thinning into a hard line. The last thing he wanted was for things to get awkward right before she met his grandfather.

When they reached his room, the lights were dimmed and a tall, thin figure lay still on the bed. How could Joshua not have noticed how frail his grandfather had gotten?

"If he's asleep, I don't want to wake him," Angie whispered.

While he felt bad that she had come all this way only to go back, he agreed with her about not waking his grandfather. "I'm sorry—"

"Oh, for God's sake. Stop with the whispering and get in here," the old man said, raising his bed into a sitting position. "I'm sulking, not sleeping."

Smiling with relief, Joshua walked up to his bedside. "How are you feeling?"

"Fit as a fiddle," he boomed as though the volume of his voice was proof of his stellar health. "Why wasn't I discharged? I don't need to be kept in the damn hospital anymore."

"Not according to your doctor," Joshua reminded him. "Besides, you won't be in the hospital much longer. We're checking you into a wellness resort tomorrow."

"Your mother told me about that. Why do I have to go to some hoity-toity retreat?" his grandfather grumbled.

"The doctor said you need absolute peace and relaxation," he said. "If you went home, nothing will keep you from going right back to work."

"What work?" Mr. Shin threw his hands up. "I'm retired."

Joshua huffed an incredulous laugh. "You're still a member of the board of directors, and you know more about what's going on in the company than any of us."

"The CEO appointment is only a few months away. With Nathan Whitley sniffing around, somebody has to keep watch," his grandfather said. "He might already have Richard Benson and Scott Grey in his pocket."

"Leave Whitley to me," Joshua said, his tone straddling confidence and arrogance. He needed to reassure his grandfather. He would deal with losing two board members to his competition later. "The board knows that I'm the best man for the job."

"Even so, you better watch your back, son. Whitley is a wily son of a bitch."

"I got this, Halabuji. You need to stop worrying and concentrate on getting better."

"Easier said than done," the old man sighed then caught sight of Angie standing quietly by the door. "And who might you be? Are you his girlfriend? Tell the boy to stop being a smart-ass."

"No, I'm not his girlfriend." She laughed, walking up to the bed. "And I'm not sure he'll take kindly to me calling him a smart-ass."

"This is Angie Han, the cellist for the Hana Trio," Joshua said, the tips of his ears burning. "She's here to play for you."

"Angie Han? Well, let me shake your hand." He took her outstretched hand with both of his. "It is an absolute pleasure to meet you. Your playing is transcendent."

"That's so kind of you to say," she said, a lovely blush spreading on her cheeks.

"She'll be coming to play for you a couple times a week," Joshua said. "But only if you're a good patient."

"Such insolence," he muttered affectionately before turning his attention back to Angie. "And how did I get so lucky as to have an accomplished cellist provide me with live music?"

"I..." She shot a quick glance at Joshua, and he gave a subtle shake of his head. Even his grandfather didn't know about his work as A.S. "I went to school with your grandson, and he looked me up for this lovely opportunity to play for you."

"The doctor thinks listening to her play will help with your recovery, Halabuji."

"Who am I to argue with the doctor?" His grandfather's twinkling eyes belied his innocent expression.

"Yes, you're the picture of a compliant patient," Joshua said drolly.

Angie watched their exchange with a smile. "Where should I set up?"

He moved a chair to the foot of the bed, leaving plenty of space for the cello. "Is this okay?"

"Yup." She lowered herself into the seat and took her cello out of the case. "Any requests?"

"I'm going to write a full list," Mr. Shin said with a contented sigh. "But for tonight, you pick for me, my dear."

"Why don't you play something short tonight?" Joshua suggested after a brief glance at his watch. "It's getting late. You can start full sessions next time."

"That works for me." After briefly tuning her cello, Angie lowered her bow to the strings. "It isn't a traditional piece but this song always warms my heart."

Joshua recognized it immediately. It was the theme from *Cinema Paradiso*, an Italian film from the eighties. The romance and heartbreak of the story had always made Angie cry. But the ripe, full sound of the notes vibrating on her cello reminded him that she was no longer the college girl he'd fallen in love with. He couldn't stop himself from wondering who this grown-up Angie really was.

He steered his mind away from the dangerous turn of thoughts and focused on the music that filled the room. The tender affection she infused into the dulcet melody made the piece hauntingly beautiful, and the intimacy of her performance seeped under his skin. The remnants of his anger toward her seemed to drain out of him. How could he stay angry at a person who could create something so lovely?

After a sweeping climax, Angie brought the song to an end. Only then was Joshua able to tear his gaze away from her. His grandfather's eyes were red with unshed tears as he clapped.

"My dear, I think you've stolen my heart," the old man said in a raspy voice.

"Thank you so much, Mr. Shin." Angie's eyes softened with fondness.

"Stop this Mr. Shin nonsense. Call me Ed."

"I can't call you by your first name," Angie gasped as though she was scandalized. Joshua couldn't hold back his grin. "I may be a second-generation Korean American, but respecting elders has been ingrained in me. If my mom were alive, she'd have my hide if I called you Ed."

Her mother had passed away? When did that happen? Angie had been so close to her mother. It must've been hard for her. Joshua's heart clenched as he imagined her loss before he caught himself. *Relax.* It was human nature to feel sympathy for someone's loss of a family member. It wasn't personal.

"Mr. Shin is so stiff and distancing," his grandfather protested. "Call me Halabuji, then."

"Okay... Halabuji." She packed up her cello and came to stand by his bed. "I'll leave you to rest."

"Good night, my dear. I'll be counting the minutes until I can hear you play again."

His grandfather's presence had eased the tension between them, but it returned in full force as they made their way out of the hospital.

"You don't need to walk me to my car," she said, breaking the silence.

"Just humor me." It was dark outside and the few streetlamps hardly lit up the parking lot.

"So...what did you think?" She glanced at him as they walked in step with each other. "Do you think I'll be able to help your grandfather?"

"He hadn't stopped complaining for a single minute since we admitted him to the hospital," he said, shaking his head. "One song from you, and he was nearly weeping with joy. So, yes. I think you'll be a huge help."

"I hope so. He's such a lovely man."

"Only when he wants to be." Joshua grinned. "He can be an utter pain in the ass."

Angie laughed. "Well, I hope I stay in his good graces."

"I don't think you'll have any trouble there," he said softly. He'd forgotten how much he liked the sound of her laughter.

"This is me." To his surprise, she stopped by a small car that was showing its age.

She'd parked under a streetlamp and the soft light shone down on her. She was so beautiful. Joshua's hands suddenly shook with the need to touch her. Was he out of his mind? *He needed to turn around and go to his car* but his feet wouldn't obey, so he continued standing in front of Angie like a rooted tree.

Without premeditation, he stuck his hand out toward her. She blinked in surprise then hesitantly placed her warm hand into his. An electric jolt rocked his entire body and his hand tightened around hers. He swallowed with difficulty. A small tug and she would be in his arms. Temptation sang in his head. He was playing with fire. Gathering every ounce of his self-control, he released her hand and turned on his heel.

It was only when he was driving home that he realized he hadn't even said good-night to her.

Three

Angie marveled at the view of the sun setting over the sparkling azure ocean as she drove to the Malibu retreat where Mr. Shin was recuperating. The stunning sunset distracted her from her nervousness about seeing Joshua again. He probably wouldn't be there anyway. Why would he visit his grandfather at the same time she did? Besides, what was she even going to do if he came? *Ogle him*. She sighed, growing impatient with herself.

Once she arrived at the resort, she walked across the beautifully manicured lawn and signed herself in at the reception desk. Then she was shown to a private cottage a short walk from the main building.

"Angie." Mr. Shin spread his arms out in welcome from a recliner by the window. "Please come in."

“Hello, Halabuji,” she said as she walked into the spacious living room.

There was a gorgeous view of the ocean and a hint of lavender in the air. But no Joshua. She quelled the disappointment rising inside her. A music stand and chair had already been set up, so she sat down and pulled out her cello.

Joshua had thawed toward her that night at the hospital, and she was hoping maybe they could… Could what? Be friends? Her heart sank. She realized she wanted him back in her life. But how would that be possible?

“You seem distracted tonight,” Mr. Shin said, concern clouding his kind eyes. “Is everything all right?”

“Of course,” she quickly reassured him. “I’m just a little tired, but I promise to be one hundred percent focused when I play for you.”

“I don’t doubt that. You’re a professional through and through. But you can play a short piece and head on home. You should get some rest.”

“No, I’m fine.” She put some pep in her voice. “Joshua sent me your list and I want to get started on it. You picked one of my favorites for the first piece.”

Before Mr. Shin could object some more, Angie lowered her bow to the strings. Her heart went into the poignant melody and she lost herself in the music. It wasn’t until she finished playing that she saw him leaning against the doorframe.

“Joshua?” Her heart pumped with sudden vigor. He was only there to visit his grandfather. His appearance had nothing to do with her. Still, her heart wouldn't quiet. "I didn't see you there."

"That was the goal. I didn't want to disturb you while you were playing." He pushed himself away from the doorway and walked over to his grandfather. "How are you feeling today, Halabuji?"

"Like I can climb a mountain," Mr. Shin said with a stubborn set of his jaw. "I don't know why you all have me locked up in here."

Angie bit her cheek to stop the laughter from bubbling up. He had been all smiles when she came in, looking well rested and in good spirits. He was just giving his grandson a hard time.

"You're hardly locked up. Mom and Dad visit almost every day," Joshua said in a gentle voice. Warmth glowed in her chest at how good he was to his grandfather. "And they told me you took a nice long walk today. The grounds here are beautiful."

"I'm trying to make the best of my rotten situation." Mr. Shin sniffed and eased back against the recliner. He was really laying it on thick.

"Rotten situation?" Joshua waved his arm to encompass the lovely room and view. "I wouldn't mind staying here for a few weeks."

"Then you stay," Mr. Shin muttered before yawning loudly. "I'm calling it an early night. Be sure to walk Angie to her car."

"Of course." Joshua spoke before Angie could protest, then stood uncertainly for a moment. "I guess it's good night, then?"

"Good night," the older man said decisively, dismissing his grandson for the night.

"Rest well, Halabuji." She kissed his cheek. "I'll see you next week."

"I can't wait. Your visits make all this nonsense more tolerable." He squeezed her hand once and let go. "Now go and get some rest. You've been tired since you got here."

When Joshua's eyes shot to her, she instinctively let her hair fall forward to hide her face and walked out of the cottage. He fell into step beside her, shortening his stride to keep pace with her.

"Is what he said true?" He glanced sideways at her as they walked past the main building.

"Practicing and performing at endless functions is exhausting," she said with a shrug. It was the truth, but she also had no intention of revealing that the source of her distraction wasn't exhaustion but him. "But performing in person is a privilege, so I can't complain."

"Are you sure you're not overdoing it?"

"Overdoing it?" She arched an eyebrow. "Thank you for your concern, but I'm fully capable of deciding how much and how hard I work. It's my career and my life, after all."

"I'm not trying to overstep any boundaries," he snapped. "I just don't want you to worry my grandfather like you did tonight."

"Worry him? Of all the arrogant, overbearing..." She clamped her mouth shut and took a deep breath. He was worried about his grandfather, but she refused to let him accuse her of causing harm to Mr. Shin.

"Your grandfather is a wise, astute man who has the insight to understand that people sometimes get tired in this modern world. He won't worry himself over my occasional yawns. But if you think I'm a harmful influence on his health, then I'll stop coming to see him, and you can reconsider your *price*."

Joshua rubbed his face in frustration. "I never said you were a harmful influence on him."

"Then what *are* you saying?" She stopped walking and turned to him.

"I'm saying it will benefit everyone if you took better care of yourself," he said in a softer tone, taking a step toward her. "You used to get so lost in your music, you wouldn't even eat until I reminded you."

"Well, that was a long time ago," she said, the animosity draining from her. "I'm a grown woman and I can take care of myself."

Something flared in his eyes at her words and he took yet another step toward her. A shiver ran down her back, and her pulse quickened. The heat from their argument turned into heat of an entirely different nature. Panic and anticipation rose in her, and she couldn't decide whether to step away from him or toward him.

"You're right." His voice was a husky drawl and his fingers grazed her cheek as he tucked a strand of hair behind her ear. "You are a grown woman."

She fought the urge to press his hand against her face and breathe in his scent. Ripping herself out of the trance, she spun away from him and resumed her trek toward her car. After a pause, Joshua was by her side, walking in step with her. To both her relief and disappointment, they arrived at her car much too soon.

"I scored a parking spot super close to the main building," she babbled, flustered by her reaction to him.

"What happened to your sexy red Boxster?" He cocked his head to the side and looked at her semi-compact curiously.

Her heart lurched and she frantically searched for an answer that wouldn't reveal her independence from her father. She couldn't divulge that to Joshua without him asking more questions, because she'd led him to believe that she left him so her father wouldn't cut her off.

Couldn't she just tell him the truth? Tell him that her father had pressured her to leave him, using her mom's cancer diagnosis to guilt her into compliance? No, she couldn't. How could she tell him that after all this time? What would be the point? It wasn't going to change what happened. Besides, he probably wouldn't believe her. She would only humiliate herself.

"It was a childish indulgence," she said, steadying her cello case against the car door. "That thing was a gas guzzler. Very environmentally irresponsible."

"Hmm," he murmured, clearly not sold on her excuse.

"Why are you here tonight?" Angie blurted to change the subject. "I thought… I thought you visited your grandfather in the mornings."

"I had an early-morning meeting today, so I wasn't able to visit him earlier."

"Oh, I see," she said in a small voice, feeling like a fool for being disappointed. What had she expected him to say? That he'd come tonight because he wanted to see her? "Then I guess I won't be seeing you for a while."

"Why do I get the feeling you're relieved?" he said with a crooked smile. "Maybe I'll schedule more meetings in the morning so I can come visit my grandfather in the evenings. I think listening to you play will do me some good as well."

He was teasing her. Maybe even laughing at her. Did he enjoy seeing her flustered? Or had he guessed the reason behind her discomfort? Well, she wasn't giving him the satisfaction of seeing how much he affected her.

"Suit yourself." She shrugged.

They stood awkwardly for a moment, neither of them speaking. She wondered if he was about to offer to shake her hand like the last time. Angie hadn't been able to stop thinking about the warmth of his touch and the jolt of awareness that had run through her that night. It wasn't wise but she wanted to touch him again.

She stuck her hand out to him, her chest rising and falling quicker than warranted for an offer of a handshake. "Good night, then."

He stared down at her outstretched hand for a moment too long, his expression unreadable. Angie was about to pull her hand back as mortification welled in her when his hand shot out to envelop hers. Her eyes locked with his. He still didn't say a word, but she shivered at the intensity of his gaze. Lust, raw and wild, pooled at her center, and she stepped toward him without thought until she stood within inches of him.

"Joshua," she whispered, not knowing what she was asking for.

His arm circled her waist and pulled her flush against his body. Her breath left her in a rush and his eyes—hungry and wild—dropped to her lips. Time stilled and the world around them faded. All that mattered was being in his arms with her hands pressed against his hard chest with the feel of his thundering heart beneath them.

But as suddenly as he'd embraced her, he released her and stepped back—once then twice. She searched his face but the impenetrable mask had slid back in place. After another moment, he spun on his heel and left her by her car. Bewildered as she was, all she could think was whether he would always walk away from her without saying *good-night.*

Joshua stared unseeingly at his computer screen as his thoughts turned to the other night at the wellness resort. Once again, he hadn't said good-night to Angie. Why was it so hard to remember to utter two damn syllables? In his defense, he'd needed to get away from her before he pushed her up against her car and ravished her. How could he have lost his mind like that?

Without him realizing it, the hurt and anger of losing her all those years ago had receded into the background to be replaced by a desperate need to know her. To discover who she was all over again.

But he would be a fool to trust her. In a way, Angie had irrevocably altered the course of his life when she left him. In college, he had spurned his family's legacy and dedicated himself to music—all but severing his relationship with his father. But after everything he'd sacrificed, he had lost his music when he lost her. It was as though he had ceased to exist.

It had taken him six long years to be able to compose again. By then, he had joined Riddle Incorporated, following his father's wishes. He learned the true value of the legacy his grandfather and father had built, and knew he would never turn his back on Riddle.

So he decided to compose in secret as A.S. to save his father from the unnecessary worry that he might choose music over Riddle again. Especially since Joshua didn't know whether he would make it as a composer—his confidence was shot after being unable to compose for six years. He and his father had only begun to mend their relationship...he didn't want to risk another rift over something he might ultimately fail at.

But now, his secret hung over him like a dark cloud, threatening his family's legacy. With the CEO appointment so close, it was more vital than ever to hide his identity as A.S. to keep Riddle out of Nathan Whitley's reach.

And ever since Angie came back into his life, he hadn't been able to compose a single note. This time felt different from when he'd lost her, though. Back then there was only cold silence but now the music was just jumbled up inside him, looking for a way out. Could his conflicted feelings toward her be stifling his creativity? Did he need to distance himself or get closer to her to free himself of his creative block?

Joshua dropped his head toward his desk and squeezed the back of his neck. He'd visited his grandfather this morning so he wouldn't be tempted to return in the evening—when Angie was there—but he couldn't get any work done. Foolish or not, all he could think about was seeing her again. He couldn't run from this. From her. They needed to talk about what was happening between them like adults, even though he still had no idea what to make of it.

He pushed away from the desk and strode out of his office. He glanced at his watch and tapped his foot as he waited for the elevators. It was past seven o'clock and the parking structure was nearly empty. With his heart hammering inside him, he drove his car onto the street. When he realized he was pushing eighty miles per hour, he eased his foot off the pedal and took a deep breath through his nose. He was rushing to the wellness resort as though he couldn't wait to see her. He needed to stop acting like some lovesick kid.

When he arrived at his grandfather's cottage, Halabuji gave him an all-knowing smirk. "To what do I owe the honor of this second visit today?"

Joshua picked up a meditation book from a side table and flipped through it. "I've been so busy with work lately. I figured I can use some music therapy, too."

"So you decided to crash my therapy session?" He chuckled. "Why not? Let's make it a music therapy party."

"We're having a party?" Angie asked from the doorway, her gaze lingering on Joshua for a second. "I'll be happy to provide the music."

"Welcome, my dear," his grandfather greeted her happily.

"Hello, Halabuji." She came up to him and placed a light kiss on his weathered cheek. "How are you feeling today?"

"Fine. I always feel fine." The old man patted her hand. "But with you here, I feel great."

"Flatterer," she said with a teasing smile then turned to Joshua. "I didn't expect to see you today. Another early morning meeting?"

His grandfather jumped in before Joshua could come up with an excuse. "No, this is his second visit of the day. He thinks he needs music therapy, too."

"Is that so?" she murmured, glancing at Joshua from under her lashes.

He tugged his tie loose and cleared his throat. "There's nothing like good music after a long day."

"Hmm." She cocked her head as though she didn't quite believe him. "I'll gladly play for both of you. What's next on your list, Halabuji?"

His grandfather pulled out a piece of paper from his back pocket and put on his reading glasses. He traced the list with one finger, muttering as he read.

"Ah, yes," he said at last. "Today's piece is the Allegro in Dvorak's Cello Concerto in B Minor. I'm very excited for this one."

Joshua's gaze shot to Angie and their eyes met. It was the piece she had played for him the night they first made love. From the deep blush staining her cheeks, she was remembering that night just as he was.

"It's one of my favorite pieces, too," she said with a touch of huskiness in her quiet voice. "But it isn't the most relaxing piece. Are you sure this is the right song for you right now?"

"Absolutely. It'll be like an extra dose of vitamins to invigorate me. I hope you won't tone it down on my account."

"I won't be able to even if I tried." She smiled, raising her bow. "You'll get the real deal. Don't worry."

She played the piece with her entire body, making strands of long hair slip out of her ponytail. Even when she opened her eyes, Joshua didn't think she saw the room or its occupants. She was completely absorbed in the performance, and her strength and passion pulsed through the music.

It was beautiful. She was beautiful. And he wanted her.

It wasn't wise. No, it was downright reckless. They'd been down this road before. She'd cast aside their love to secure her trust fund. No matter how much he wanted to know this grown-up Angie, he couldn't trust her. She had her priorities and he wasn't one of them. Not only that, but her presence in his life was interfering with his ability to compose. He couldn't risk losing his music again.

His grandfather's resounding applause snapped Joshua out of his frantic thoughts, and he belatedly applauded Angie for her amazing performance.

"I'll never forget tonight's performance," the old man said when she came to stand next to him. "You are a gift to the world and to me."

"Thank you, Halabuji," she said, the corners of lips wobbling. "All I want is for you to get well. I hope my music is helping you feel better."

"It is. I haven't felt this alive since I was a young man."

"Good. Just keep that up while we go through your list, okay?"

"I will, my dear." He clasped Angie's hand and squeezed. "Thank you."

"It is my absolute pleasure," she whispered with a catch in her voice.

Joshua stood watching the scene with his heart in a vise, and he couldn't help but think about what could've been. Would they have gotten married? Would Angie have been his grandfather's granddaughter-in-law if she hadn't left him? He impatiently brushed aside the thought.

"It's time for you to rest," he said, placing a hand on his grandfather's shoulder.

He covered Joshua's hand with his. "I will. I promised Angie I'll get better soon."

"You bet you did." Angie smiled and glanced at Joshua. "Are you leaving?"

"Yes, I'll walk you to your car," he said. "Good night, Halabuji."

They left the cottage and walked across the lawn in subdued silence. The resonance of the song and the memories it brought to the surface still clung heavily to him. But now that he had her to himself, he couldn't think of anything to say.

"Do you want a cup of coffee?" he blurted when they got to her car. He wasn't ready to let her go. "There's a decent coffee shop a couple blocks from here."

She hesitated for a second before giving him a small smile. "Sure. That sounds nice."

He grinned so broadly in response that his cheeks cramped. He had no idea where this was headed, but he would settle for her company. That was enough. For now.

Four

Joshua still hadn't kissed her. He hadn't even mentioned their near kiss. She was fine with that. If he wanted to pretend that nothing happened, so could she.

She watched him from beneath her lashes as she sipped her coffee. He often visited his grandfather in the evenings, which led to more trips to the coffee shop and interesting conversations. Like tonight. They mostly talked about music. He still shared that passion with her and sometimes sounded wistful about not being able to fully dedicate his time to it.

Angie enjoyed these interludes with him, but she didn't know what to make of their current situation. Were they friends now? He might think they were headed down that path, but she didn't necessarily feel friendly toward him. Beneath their light conversations, the undercurrent of their attraction swirled wildly, growing stronger each time they were together. And she wanted to kiss him. So badly.

She wasn't sure if she could stop wanting him. Did she have to, though? He didn't seem to hate her anymore. Maybe he would be willing to listen to why she really left him, and maybe even forgive her. But then what?

"Will you be open to that?" Joshua asked.

"What was that?" She'd completely missed what he'd been saying.

"I think it'll be exciting to write this new piece with the specific performers in mind. I'll work off the Hana Trio's strengths and what makes each of your sounds your own," he said, leaning forward on the table. She got a whiff of his woodsy scent, and she almost lost her concentration again. "So would you mind if I sit in on one of your practice sessions?"

"No, I don't mind..." She wrapped her hands around her mug.

"But?" he prompted.

"But we need to keep your identity a secret from my sisters, right?"

"Right."

"How are we going to do that?" She worried her bottom lip. "I don't want to lie point-blank to my sisters."

"Hmm." He sat back with his chin in his hand. "How about if you tell them that you have an eccentric donor who wants to observe one of your rehearsals? You won't be lying to them. I did donate to the Chamber Music Society."

"And you happen to be very eccentric," she teased. It was strange to feel comfortable enough to joke around with him. It certainly wasn't like the *old days*, but they'd built an unexpected rapport.

He chuckled, and she stared at the way his eyes crinkled at the corners. Laugh lines were beginning to form, and she loved seeing the evidence of his happiness on his face. No matter how much she'd hurt him in the past, he'd had a happy life. He certainly had smiled and laughed a lot in the past ten years.

"So will you set something up?" he asked expectantly.

"Will next Wednesday morning work for you?"

"I'll make it work." He grinned widely at her, and her heart did a little flip-flop.

To cover her reaction to him, she took a sip of her coffee and promptly choked on it.

"Are you okay?" He came to stand beside her and moved his warm hand up and down her back in soothing strokes.

"Yes, I'm fine," she gasped, blinking back tears.

"Sure, you are."

He didn't stop his ministrations until her cough subsided. Although she wanted Joshua's continued touch, she gently pushed away his hand for the sake of her sanity. When his eyes darkened at her lingering glance at his lips, she was tempted to throw caution to the wind. He was still leaning over her, near enough to kiss. She could just grab him right here and now. Before she did something she would regret, she pushed back her chair, forcing him to step back.

"I should be getting home," she announced and stood awkwardly as Joshua continued to stare at her.

After what felt like an eternity, he murmured, "Let me walk you to your car."

"So who is this mystery patron?" Chloe demanded as soon as she stepped into the practice room.

"All she told me was that his name was Joshua Shin." Megan brought their little sister up to speed, having arrived a few minutes earlier. "She won't spill anything else about him."

"Because there isn't anything to spill." Angie threw up her hands, getting flustered by her sisters' curiosity. "He just wants to watch us practice. He's going to sit somewhere in the corner and disturb us as little as possible."

"Like watching endangered gorillas in their natural habitat," Chloe chortled.

"We're on exhibit every time we perform. What's the big deal about having someone sit in on one of our rehearsals?" Angie said.

Yeah, what's the big deal? Why was she so nervous about having Joshua at their practice? Well, she hated keeping secrets from her sisters. But it wasn't only about keeping A.S.'s identity a secret—she couldn't let them find out about her history with Joshua, either.

If Megan and Chloe ever discovered that their father had made Angie choose between their dying mother and Joshua, it would completely disillusion them about their father. It was one thing for her to be estranged from their father, but that didn't mean she wanted him to be isolated from all his children. He hadn't been the same since their mother died. He needed her sisters, and they needed him, too.

And there was something else. Joshua watching her practice was much too intimate. She didn't want to show him too much of her real self—her frustration over missing a note, her triumph at playing a section perfectly for the first time and her interactions with her sisters, whom she loved so much. She couldn't say why, but she had a feeling that it was very important to keep a part of herself hidden from him.

"It actually isn't a big deal...for us," Meg said shrewdly, "but something is going on with you, because you don't even get this anxious before a concert."

"But it's kind of fun watching our perfect older sister lose her cool for once," Chloe interjected.

"I am not losing my cool," Angie said through clenched teeth. She *was* losing her cool, and her sisters were getting more suspicious by the minute.

Just then Joshua walked into the room, wearing an impeccable gray pinstripe suit and a royal blue tie. There was a stunned silence as both her sisters—and she—absorbed the impact of his presence.

"Hello, ladies," he said with a hint of a smile.

"Hel-loooo, Joshua Shin," Chloe said with a cheeky smirk aimed at Angie.

"Chloe," Megan whisper-screamed. "That is so inappropriate...but I feel you, sister."

"Welcome, Mr. Shin." Angie walked up to him with her hand outstretched before her sisters embarrassed her any further. "We're so happy to have you here. May I introduce you to my sisters? This is Megan Han, our violinist."

"Nice to meet you, Mr. Shin," Megan said formally.

"And Chloe is our violist," Angie continued.

"That's me." Their youngest sister waved cheerily.

"It's a privilege to meet you both," Joshua said with a charming smile. "I'm a fan of the Hana Trio. And I'm thrilled to be a fly on the wall at your rehearsal."

"Do you and Angie already know each other?" Chloe glanced back and forth between them.

"Yes, we went to college together," he stated matter-of-factly.

Angie wanted to groan out loud. Her sisters were going to bombard her with more questions once the practice was over. "Mr. Shin is not here to chitchat with us. He came to hear us practice, so let's practice."

"Mr. Shin? Why so formal?" Megan asked. "I thought you were college buddies."

"We were *not* buddies," Angie said, taking her cello out of its case. It was the truth. She and Joshua had been lovers, not friends.

Her sisters exchanged a glance that she didn't trust at all, but they both took their seats and prepared their instruments. Joshua lowered himself into a chair in the corner of the room. They were practicing a relatively new piece and still had a lot of kinks to work out. Angie fleetingly wished they were working on a more polished piece, but this was a practice session not a performance.

She quickly tuned her cello and played an open A for her sisters. Her eyes flittered once or twice to where Joshua was sitting, but she forced herself to focus on the rehearsal.

"From the top?" Megan asked as she raised her bow.

"Yes, we need to work on the opening bars," Chloe said with a determined look on her face.

They practiced the opening for the next hour, playing the same few bars again and again. They weren't delivering a unified sound, and they grew more and more determined to get it right. This rehearsal probably wasn't exactly what Joshua was hoping for. But when her worried glance met his, he gave her a reassuring smile.

When she and her sisters finally got the opening down, the music flowed more smoothly and they ended the practice on a high note.

"Chloe, you were busting our ass today," Megan said, beaming with pride.

"The opening is so important with this piece. I wanted us to get it just right." Chloe smiled shyly.

"And we did it, girls." Angie high-fived her sisters.

The sound of applause interrupted their celebration. They'd been so absorbed in their practice that they'd forgotten Joshua was in the room with them.

"That was amazing," he said, walking up to them. "Thank you for allowing me to observe. It was an honor."

“Wow, thank you.” Chloe clasped her hands over her chest and mouthed to Angie, *Oh, my God.*

“Yeah, thanks. Come back *anytime*,” Megan said magnanimously, earning a warning glare from Angie.

“Let me walk you out, Mr. Shin.” Angie didn’t give him a chance to respond before ushering him out of the room—away from her incorrigible sisters.

“Sorry about my sisters,” she said once they were standing in the parking lot. “They’re usually more professional, but the practice room is kind of our safe space where anything goes. I guess it’s hard to turn on the professionalism in there.”

“I enjoyed meeting them.” Joshua smiled warmly at her. “The three of you seem close.”

“We are close, and I love working with them,” she said, returning his smile. “I don’t know if listening to us play the same few bars over and over again helped, but I hope you got what you needed from our rehearsal.”

“I did. It was incredible watching you and your sisters work together to find the perfect sound.”

When he reached out and took her hand in his, it felt like the most natural thing for her to squeeze it.

“Thank you,” she whispered.

“I should let you get back to them,” he said, his thumb skimming the top of her hand. “I’ll see you tonight.”

“Yeah.” Her heart fluttered helplessly inside her. “See you tonight.”

He released her hand reluctantly, his fingertips lingering on her skin. Without thinking, she grabbed his arm before he could walk away. His eyebrows rose in surprise and he searched her face. Whatever he saw there made fire light in his eyes. With a muttered curse, he crushed his mouth against hers.

This was what she wanted. She sighed a long-held breath and invited him in. His tongue dove into her mouth, drawing a deep moan from her. His kiss was full of hunger, bewilderment and desperation, and she answered in kind. They shouldn't be doing this, but she had missed it so. She rose on her toes and pulled his head down, wanting him to kiss her harder. He obliged with a guttural groan, fisting a hand in her hair to tilt her head to the side.

She pushed her hands inside his suit jacket and spread them flat on his chest, reveling in the feel of him. His arms came around her back and pulled her flush against him, trapping her hands between them. His hard length pushed against her stomach and made her melt into him.

"Angie." Longing saturated his voice, turning her name into the single most intimate word he could utter.

Then she froze. She wanted to take him with an urgency that made her light-headed. But they were in the middle of a parking lot in broad daylight. She belatedly heard the snickers and whispers of passersby and blushed to her roots.

Joshua sighed against her lips and drew back. He gently brushed a strand of hair away from her face and gave her a rueful smile. When she glanced down at her toes with an embarrassed laugh, he lifted her chin with his finger.

"As I was saying," his eyes gleamed with promise, "I'll see you tonight."

The evening traffic in Los Angeles was at its most obnoxious. Joshua leaned back in his seat and drummed his fingers on the steering wheel in time with the music. He didn't mind enjoying the anticipation humming through him a while longer. He was going to see Angie soon.

The kiss they shared earlier today had been nothing like the sweet, tender kisses they'd shared before, even in the throes of passion. It had been raw, frantic and hot as fuck. He remembered with vivid clarity the feel of her lips crushed beneath his and her tongue sparring with his. And God, the little whimpering noises she made had driven him wild. Desire flared through his body at the memory and his blood rushed south.

He shook his head to clear it. The chemistry between them was undeniable but he couldn't forget her betrayal. The more time he spent with her, the harder it was to remember that she had once broken his heart. He couldn't make himself vulnerable to her again no matter how much he wanted her.

Then there was his music. Watching her practice with her sisters this morning had been remarkable. Their single-minded determination to reach the truest sound had sparked inspiration in him and he'd begun to hear the whispers of music in his mind. It had still been formless and scattered, but he'd sensed the start of something beautiful. But now all was quiet. The conflict between his desire and mistrust for Angie twisted his insides and suffocated his creativity. Even if he could risk his heart again, he couldn't risk his music.

But despite it all, he couldn't forget how right she'd felt in his arms and he grew impatient to see her. It was madness but he was helpless against her pull on him. His cell phone rang as he dragged his fingers through his hair. Panic constricted his chest when he saw that it was the wellness resort. He brushed aside his irrational reaction and answered the call.

"This is Joshua Shin."

"Mr. Shin," said a woman in a too-tranquil voice. It made him clench his jaws tighter. "Your grandfather was having trouble breathing and was just transported to the emergency room."

"Which hospital?" he asked as dread seeped into his veins.

His mind remained stark and empty with fear as he rushed to the hospital. He screeched into the first parking spot he found and shot out of his car. He ran the last stretch to the emergency room.

"Angie?" He came to a stop when he saw her pacing in front of the entrance.

"Joshua." She reached his side with hurried steps.

"Where's my grandfather? What's happening to him?" He walked past Angie and spun around the waiting area as though his grandfather was hiding somewhere.

"The paramedics were taking Mr. Shin away when

I arrived at the wellness resort. I followed them here, but they won't let me see him since I'm not family." She came to stand beside him and gathered his cold hands between her own. "I let them know you were on your way."

He stalked to the front desk. "I need to see Edward Shin *now.* I'm his grandson."

The receptionist smiled sympathetically at him even though he was acting like a brute and typed into the computer. "I believe a doctor is attending to him at the moment. We'll update you as soon as we know more, sir."

He blew out a frustrated breath and pushed his fingers through his hair. Before he could make more unreasonable demands, Angie appeared at his side. "Why don't we go sit down?"

Joshua suddenly didn't know what he should do and turned lost eyes to her. She took hold of his hand again and found seats at the back of the crowded waiting area. His thoughts ran in circles and the only thing anchoring him was the firm pressure of Angie's hand holding his. They sat and waited like that for over an hour.

"Edward Shin's family?" The woman at the front desk scanned the crowded room. "Edward Shin's family?"

Joshua shot to his feet and bounded up to her. "Yes. I'm here."

"Your grandfather has been moved to the ICU. The doctor there will be able to tell you more."

"The ICU? What does that mean?" he demanded. "I need to know..."

"Thank you," Angie interjected, putting a calming hand on his arm. He clamped his mouth shut and inhaled through his nose. "How do we get to the ICU?"

After thanking the receptionist once more, Angie started walking and he followed her without question. They stepped outside into the evening air, then eventually entered an adjacent building.

"Let's go sit in the waiting room," she said after they checked in at the nurses' station. He nodded numbly.

She guided him into a long, rectangular room with cushioned chairs and watercolor paintings adorning the walls. When she stopped in front of some chairs in the corner, he sat down, his posture rigid. His grandfather was ill. He shouldn't be sitting. He should be *doing* something.

"There's nothing you can do right now," Angie said softly as though she'd read his mind. "Try to rest a little."

"I should call my parents." Or should he? They were in New York for their anniversary, and he didn't want to disturb them. But if their positions were reversed, he would want to know as soon as possible.

Angie nodded and stepped out of the room, leaving him alone. Despite his decision to call them, his fingers wouldn't press the dial button right away. It had required much convincing for them to take the trip. They were too worried to go far from Halabuji, but he'd been doing so well lately. This call was going to worry them, but he hoped they wouldn't feel too guilty. Muttering a curse under his breath, he pressed Dial.

"Joshua." His mother answered after two rings even though it was past midnight there. "Is everything okay?"

"Mom." He paused to swallow the lump in his throat. "Halabuji is in the ICU."

"Oh, my God. I knew we shouldn't have left him," she said, panic rising in her voice.

"Please don't blame yourself. You couldn't have known. And I'm here," he reassured her. "I'm waiting to speak with the doctor, so I'll let you know when I know more. For the time being, try not to worry too much."

"Who is that? Is something wrong?" Joshua heard his father murmur by his mother's side.

"Honey, it's your father. He's in the hospital," she said to him.

There was a flurry of noise on the other end of the line. His father must have jumped out of bed.

"Your dad's on the phone with the airline. We'll book a flight out of here as soon as we can," she said. "How are you holding up?"

"I'm just impatient to speak with the doctor." He sidestepped her question. "Halabuji is strong. He'll pull through this just fine."

"I know he will," she said with quiet conviction. "I'll see you soon."

"Fly safe, Mom."

Joshua sat alone in the waiting room for a few minutes before Angie returned holding two paper cups.

"I went down to the café and got you a decaf green tea." She handed him a cup. "I figured you didn't need to add caffeine into the mix."

"Thank you." He offered her a small smile. He didn't know how he would have made it through this without her. If it wasn't for her calming presence, he might still be rampaging around the hospital demanding to see his grandfather.

"Of course." She settled down next to him.

"You know, you don't need to stay with me," he said, hoping she wouldn't leave.

"I know." She sipped her coffee and made no move to go.

His shoulders slumped in relief, and he leaned back against his chair. But the reprieve was short-lived as his mind churned with anxiety and frustration. Was his grandfather fighting for his life in there? Then he should be with him. His grandfather shouldn't be in there alone. The vise clenched around his heart squeezed harder.

He started when Angie placed her hand on his knee. Despite everything, instant heat spread through his body at her touch. Lost for words, he raised his eyebrows in question.

"Your knee was jumping around so hard that it was creating a small earthquake. I was afraid I might spill my coffee." Her lips curved upward in a gentle smile, and her eyes were warm with sympathy.

"I'm sorry. I'm just…" He looked down at her hand, which was still resting on his knee.

"Getting more worried by the minute," she finished his sentence. "Where is the damn doctor anyway?"

"I'm actually right here." A fit, middle-aged woman with salt-and-pepper hair stood at the doorway with a congenial smile. "I apologize for the delay. I assume you're Edward Shin's family?"

Angie drew her hand away from Joshua's knee and he stood up to greet the doctor. "Yes, I'm his grandson. How is my grandfather?"

"He's stable for now. The good news is he didn't have another heart attack, but his heart rate was erratic and much too fast when he was brought into the ER. At one point, we had to perform emergency procedures to resuscitate him."

"Are you telling me that his heart stopped?" Joshua's voice shook.

"Yes," the doctor said bluntly. "We believe the scars from his previous heart attack contributed to his ventricular fibrillation—his irregular heart rhythm."

"How do we prevent this from happening again?" Joshua's panic receded to be replaced by determination.

"Once he recovers his strength, we need to discuss more-invasive surgery."

Joshua nodded once. He appreciated the doctor's straight talk. He didn't think he could take some roundabout, sugarcoated explanation without losing his shit. So far they had decided against invasive surgery due to his grandfather's age, but they couldn't let him go through this again.

"Can I see him?" he asked.

"He's asleep and needs absolute rest tonight. I'll allow visitations tomorrow."

"I won't wake him. I just want to see that he's all right."

"Okay." The doctor relented. "Just for five minutes."

Joshua glanced at Angie and she smiled. "Go ahead. I'll wait for you here."

The doctor showed him to his grandfather's bed and said, "Remember. Five minutes."

Joshua nodded, his eyes glued to the old man. Other than his slight pallor and the oxygen tube in his nose, Halabuji looked just as he had the night before. The fist clenched around Joshua's heart loosened its hold as he watched his grandfather's peaceful slumber.

Once he stepped out of the ICU, exhaustion rolled in. He wasn't ready to lose his grandfather. When he opened the door to the waiting room, Angie put aside the magazine she'd been flipping through and quickly crossed over to him. She put her arms around his waist and held him close, and the sob lodged in his chest almost broke free. He wrapped his arms around her and pulled her tighter against him.

"Are you okay?" she whispered against his chest.

"Yes…no. Actually, I'm not okay," he said, his voice raspy with fear and fatigue. "I'm not ready to lose him."

"Oh, Joshua. I'm sure he's not ready to leave you, either. He'll fight his way out of this."

Her warmth, her sympathy and the comfort she offered kept him from falling apart. He needed this. He needed her.

"Come home with me, Angie."

Five

Angie couldn't refuse. She didn't want to. He was hurting and she would give him all the comfort she could. Their kiss in the parking lot had lit a spark of hope inside her, but tonight wasn't about her. He needed her and she was there for him. It was as simple as that.

Joshua's condo was nothing like she'd imagined. The earth-toned walls of the living room were lined with overflowing bookshelves. There was a well-worn but welcoming beige leather sofa, and the low coffee table looked like the perfect place to rest your feet on.

But the grand piano was the centerpiece of the room. It was situated by a large window, and she could imagine Joshua looking up from it to gaze at the view of the city beyond, while thinking up the next notes of his composition.

This wasn't some sleek bachelor pad. It was his home. The space was so warm and intimate, she had a feeling that not a lot of people were invited in. When she turned toward him, he was looking intently at her.

"What do you think?" he asked with almost imperceptible hesitation. "Do you like it?"

Did it matter to him whether she liked his condo or not? A jolt of pleasure ran through her. "I love it. I'm glad you have such a wonderful place to come home to."

"Thank you." Joshua cleared his throat and pulled his tie loose. "Make yourself at home."

"Thank you," she said and sat down on the couch. It was as comfortable as it looked. She wanted to lie down on it and take a nap. But she wasn't there to nap. She was there to… What exactly was she there to do? The answer to that question made heat rush to her cheeks.

"Would you like a drink?" he asked. "Scotch?"

"Scotch sounds good."

He swiftly disappeared into the kitchen behind the living room. Before she could wonder whether he was hiding from her, he came back carrying two glasses of amber liquid. He handed her a glass and sat down on the other end of the couch. After a deep gulp, Joshua set his glass on the coffee table and ran his hands over his face. She put down her untouched drink and scooted closer to him to rub his back.

"Hey," she said softly, "I know tonight has been a lot, but everything is going to be okay."

"I know," he said, meeting her gaze with sad, lost eyes. "But knowing and believing are two different things. And a part of my mind won't stop screaming in fear."

Her heart ached for him and tears prickled at the back of her eyes. She had no more words of comfort that could change the way he felt, so she leaned forward and gave him a feather-light kiss. When he stared at her with parted lips, she kissed him again, deeper this time.

With a growl, he opened his mouth wider and traced the inside of her bottom lip with his tongue. Heat unfurled low in her stomach, and Angie struggled to get closer to him. Joshua lifted her onto his lap and deepened the kiss, tasting her like she was sweet nectar.

She whimpered in protest when he broke the kiss but was appeased when he trailed his lips along her jawline and up to the sensitive spot behind her ear. He gave her a lingering kiss there and blew softly on it. She shivered and a low, sexy chuckle rumbled in his chest. He remembered. That was the exact spot that had made her weak-kneed with lust when they were together.

"Joshua," she breathed, running her hands down his firm chest and stomach. His muscles jerked in response to her touch and it was her turn to smile. He wanted her as desperately as she wanted him.

He kissed her rough and hard, moaning against her

lips, and any reserve she might have had melted away. She shifted on his lap and moved her leg across his thighs to straddle him. He groaned as though he were in pain when she swiveled her hip over his erection.

His chest rose and fell quickly as her hands explored his body. Unsatisfied with touching him through his clothes, she impatiently undid one button after the next until she spread his shirt apart, revealing what lay underneath. He was magnificent. She'd loved his beautiful lean body when they were together, but the new grooves and ridges of his carved torso begged for her touch.

As though in a trance, she traced her finger along his well-defined abs, trailing it lower and lower to where the hair darkened and disappeared into the waistband of his pants. Desperate to see the rest of him, she reached for his belt buckle, but his hand shot out to grasp her by the wrist.

"Wait," he said in a choked voice. "You don't…you don't have to do this."

The wild fire in his eyes told her how much he wanted this, but he sat absolutely still as he waited for her answer.

"I want to do this." She leaned forward until her lips were a breath away from his. "I want you."

He wrapped his hand around the nape of her neck and kissed her with unleashed passion. His lips didn't leave hers as he stood with her in his arms and carried her to his bedroom. Then he laid her gently on his bed and lowered himself beside her.

"I want to look at you," he said, his voice husky.

She nodded and reached for her blouse but fumbled with the buttons. He squeezed her hands before bringing them down to her sides. With fast, proficient fingers, he finished unbuttoning her blouse and pushed it off her shoulders. He drew in a sharp breath and leaned down to kiss the tops of her breasts spilling out of her bra. Frantic for his touch, she unclasped her bra and threw it to the side.

"You're beautiful," he said, cupping her breast with one hand. His thumb drew soft circles around her areola until she writhed beside him. "Do you like that?"

"Yes," she hissed.

"Do you want more?"

"Please."

Sweat was beading on his forehead. It was as hard for him to hold back as it was for her to wait. So she pulled his head down to her breasts and he succumbed with a guttural groan, sucking one nipple, then the other, into his mouth.

When she reached for his belt this time, he didn't stop her, and she quickly unclasped the buckle and unzipped his pants. He assisted her by lifting his hips off the bed and she roughly stripped his pants off, leaving him in only his boxer briefs, with his arousal straining against the fabric.

He returned the favor, taking her pants off along with her panties. He froze for a moment as his eyes roamed her naked body. Her skin felt electrified under his gaze and she moaned when his warm hand connected with her skin.

His kiss was gentle and almost reverent as his hand

trailed down her side to her ass. He cupped her cheek and squeezed before he resumed his exploration of her body. With maddening slowness, he reached between her legs.

"You're so wet for me," he rasped when he finally touched the juncture between her thighs.

His lips were no longer gentle against hers as his tongue thrust into her mouth with urgency. He parted her folds with his fingers and rubbed her hypersensitive bud, making her head thrash from side to side.

"Joshua, I need… I need…"

He thrust his index finger inside her and her back arched off the bed. "Is this what you need?"

"More," she moaned.

He drew his finger in and out while his other hand continued circling her clit. She nearly came when he added a second finger inside her.

"So close. So…close…" she whimpered as she rode his hand.

"That's it, sweetheart. Come for me."

She finally fell apart at his rough command, and wave after wave of ecstasy washed over her. After laying a gentle kiss on her lips, Joshua stood and removed his boxer briefs. Even though she was still limp from her orgasm, she eyed his hard length with growing desire. When he returned to her side, sheathed in a condom, she spread her legs to welcome him.

He kissed her hard and fast as he positioned himself at her entrance, and she wrapped her legs around his waist.

"Joshua, I need you inside me."

He plunged into her, thrusting again and again until his full length was inside her. They moaned in unison, a sound of relief and satisfaction. This felt…right.

She had never experienced this *wholeness* with anyone else. But she pulled herself away from her thoughts. This might be a one-night thing. She couldn't let herself get carried away. It was just amazing sex. That was all.

"God, Angie. You feel so good," he growled as he set a slow rhythm that threatened her sanity.

She lifted her hips off the bed and urged him to quicken the pace. Looking straight into his half-hooded eyes, she panted, "I want you hard and fast."

All pretense at control shattered, Joshua drove into her, pulling himself nearly all the way out, then plunging into her again. Delicious tightness grew between her legs until she couldn't stand it anymore. Sensing she was close, he tilted her hip to create friction where she needed it most.

"Oh, God. Don't stop. Please …" she begged.

Angie didn't know how Joshua was keeping up this demanding pace, never slowing down, grunting with each push. But she didn't relent, either. She rode him hard, reaching frantically for her climax and crying out incoherently when her orgasm finally slammed into her.

Joshua continued thrusting wildly until he shouted with his own release. He collapsed on top of her, panting and slick with sweat. She could hardly breathe but she didn't care. She liked his solid weight on her, still connected to her. Before it became too much, he lifted his head, pushing onto his elbows to bear the brunt of his weight.

"Are you okay?" he asked, running the back of his fingers down her flushed cheek.

"Yes. Better than okay, actually." She stretched languidly.

"Is that so?" A cocky smile lifted the corner of his lips. "How much better?"

"I feel wonderful."

He leaned down to kiss her temple and said against her ear, "Good."

Joshua rolled off her and lay by her side. He grew quiet as he stared at the ceiling, his mind most likely traveling back to his grandfather. She laid her head on his bare chest, and wrapped her arm around his waist, pressing her body into his side.

With a long, heavy sigh, his eyes slid closed. She soon drifted off beside him, hoping he wouldn't hurt so much tomorrow. Hoping she wouldn't hurt, either. Tonight might be all she had with him and she had to be okay with that.

Joshua didn't think he would be able to sleep, but with Angie's soft, warm body curved around him, he fell into a deep, dreamless slumber. The next time he opened his eyes, dawn was peeping in through the curtains, and he couldn't recall where he was. All he had was a sense of peace and contentment.

He pulled the woman by his side closer to him, knowing she belonged right there. He smiled and sleep nearly lured him back, but his damn mind ruined it all by blasting the events of the night before into the center of his thoughts.

Angie was in his bed. His arms tightened around her without conscious thought. When they made love last night, he'd expected familiarity and comfort, but what he'd found was fierce, thrilling passion. It was something he'd never experienced with any other woman—not even with Angie in the past.

It was beautiful and…it couldn't happen again. He forced his arms to relax and slowly disentangled himself from her, not wanting to wake her. Feral possessiveness flashed through him as he watched her serene, sleeping face, but he pushed aside his feelings with cold swiftness.

He shouldn't have asked her to come home with him last night. But he'd wanted her for so long… and after the kiss in the parking lot, he didn't have the strength to resist her, especially with his world crumbling around him. And being the sweet, generous woman she was, Angie had made love to him as though she really wanted him. As though he meant something to her.

It was a mistake. This only complicated his already chaotic emotions. The very emotions that prevented him from composing. Losing his music meant losing his identity. No matter how right it felt to have her in his arms, he couldn't do this again.

He stepped into the shower and let the hot water wash over him. He was confused and…panicked. Yes, he wanted her, but if she could affect him like this with just one night together… He couldn't allow her to mean something to him again.

What was last night to her? Was it just pity sex? A one-night deal? The thought left a bitter taste in his mouth even though he'd just been telling himself that it couldn't happen again.

He dried himself off and quickly got dressed, being as quiet as possible to not wake Angie. He wasn't ready to speak to her yet. And if she woke up and so much as called his name, he would take her again. Although sneaking out made him feel like a first-rate jerk, it was for the best.

Joshua scribbled a quick note—"I have to head out. Stay as long as you need."—and placed it on his pillow. With her hair falling across her bare shoulder and her lips softly parted, she looked both beautiful and sexy as sin. If he stayed a second longer, he would kiss her awake. Drawing on the deepest reserve of his willpower, he spun on his heels and left for his office.

It was too early to visit his grandfather, so he might as well get as much work done as possible before heading to the hospital. Besides, if he wanted to put his night with Angie out of his mind, he needed to keep himself busy. Even though he'd taken a shower, her fragrance still seemed to linger on his skin and the scent of vanilla assailed his nostrils.

Enough of this nonsense. He repositioned his hands on the steering wheel and tried to focus on the road. Luckily, he'd left so early this morning, there wasn't much traffic. He made it to work in record time and lumbered into his office.

All the lights were still off because he was the first one in, but he didn't mind the dim stillness. It suited his current mood. Joshua needed to lose himself in his work. That was the only way he was going to get through this morning with his sanity intact.

He didn't realize how much time had passed until Janice peeked into his office.

"Good morning, Joshua," she said, walking up to his desk. She was wearing one of her bright floral dresses with her signature chunky jewelry. "Have you been here long? Have you had your coffee?"

"A few hours. And no coffee, thank you. I'm going to be with my grandfather for the better part of the day, so I needed to get some of the urgent work out of the way."

"Is everything okay?" Concern drew lines across her still-smooth forehead. No one would guess that she was a grandmother if it weren't for her mother-hen ways.

"He had a rough day yesterday, but things should be better today."

"Well, don't worry about a thing here," she said briskly. "I'll reschedule all your meetings for today."

"Thank you, Janice." He stood from his chair and pulled on his suit jacket. "I'll be back tonight but you'll already be gone by then, so I'll see you tomorrow."

"I wish you could take some time off to be with your grandfather, but I know you have to stay on top of things with the CEO appointment coming up. That Nathan Whitley will do anything to get an edge over you." She clucked her tongue. "Well, the board of directors aren't made up of fools. Anyone can see that you're the best man for the job."

"You might be a bit biased," he teased even as he prayed she was right. He couldn't let Whitley usurp the decades of hard work his grandfather and father had dedicated to building Riddle Incorporated.

"Maybe, but that doesn't mean I'm wrong," she said. "See you tomorrow, and don't forget to eat."

Joshua hurried to the parking structure and drove his car onto the road. Now that he didn't have work to distract him, his chest tightened with worry for his grandfather. His jaws clenched and his knuckles turned white on the steering wheel. Los Angeles traffic was never fun, but he had a hard time keeping his temper in check this morning.

When he got to the hospital, he rushed to the ICU nurses' station. "I'm here to see Edward Shin."

"Are you family?" asked the nurse, looking at him through glasses perched on her nose.

"Yes, I'm his grandson."

"Okay. Put yourself down on the visitor's list, but you'll have to wait half an hour for visiting hours to start. We have a waiting room around the corner."

"Thank you," he said, suppressing a wave of impatience.

He entered the waiting room and sat down in an empty seat. Everyone was either staring at their phone or reading a magazine. It was hardly a place for light conversation.

Joshua pulled out his phone, finding fifty new work emails as he'd expected. He passed through the unimportant ones and responded to the urgent ones. It took him a while to notice his knees bouncing and he forced himself to sit still with difficulty. He remembered how the weight of Angie's hand on his leg had quieted him. And the memory of his night with her rushed through him, leaving him warm and frustrated.

"Joshua," a quiet voice said in front of him.

He lifted his gaze to find the woman who refused to leave his thoughts all morning. He stood from his seat and cleared his throat. "What are you doing here?"

Something like hurt flitted across Angie's face, and he wanted to kick himself. "I had a feeling you might be here. I came to make sure you're okay and to hear news about your grandfather."

"He's stable enough to have visitors. I'm going to see him in a few minutes," Joshua said brusquely. "There was no need for you to come."

"No," she said, jutting out her chin. "I didn't *need* to come."

She came because she was worried about him, and he was being a complete asshole.

"Do you want…last night…" he blurted, but Angie stopped him with a hand on his arm.

"I already told you why I'm here—" she lowered her voice "—and discussing last night isn't one of the reasons. You have more pressing concerns."

"I…" He didn't know what to say…or what he wanted.

That wasn't entirely true. What he wanted was to pull her into his arms and hold her. But what if he didn't want to let go? He couldn't risk that. After what last night showed him, Joshua had to keep his distance from Angie.

"Please tell your grandfather to get well soon," she said softly and walked out of the waiting room.

Every instinct told him to hold on to her, but the last time he'd asked her to stay, she'd walked out of his life. The old hurt and anger shot to the surface as though it had never gone away. He couldn't forget her betrayal and what it had cost him. He had gone nearly six years without composing. He had lost a vital part of himself for far too long.

So he let her go. It was the only way to protect himself.

Six

"Mmm... I love *soondubu*," Chloe said after a big spoonful of the steaming hot tofu soup.

"Who doesn't?" Megan said, feasting on her own pot of soup. The individual rock pots kept the tofu soup boiling hot to the last drop.

Angie and her sisters' favorite *soondubu* spot was jam-packed as usual. They'd had to wait twenty minutes to get a table, but it was worth it. The warm, savory comfort food made her feel a little less forlorn.

Days had passed without a single text from Joshua. He obviously regretted spending the night with her, but he could've at least kept her apprised of his grandfather's condition. She held back a sigh as she stirred her soup. That wasn't fair. He and his parents were probably worried sick about Mr. Shin. Joshua couldn't be expected to worry about her right now. She just hoped he wasn't hurting too much.

Even so, she had a cold, hollow spot in her heart that refused to go away. It wasn't because they'd made love that night. She had wanted him for a long time, and when she saw he needed comfort, there'd been no reason to hold back. After all, it was only sex. It was the best sex she'd ever had in her life, but it was just sex nonetheless. Then why was she feeling this way?

"The Chamber Music Society is so excited about getting the new piece from A.S.," Chloe said, securing a piece of marinated cucumber with her chopsticks. "I can't believe he's writing a string trio for us."

"How did Janet even manage to commission him?" Megan asked. "He's in such high demand, and the man isn't exactly easy to find."

"She's been in this business for a long time." Angie dipped a spoonful of rice in her soup, avoiding her sisters' eyes. No matter how guilty she felt about keeping secrets from them, she had to protect them from the truth about their father's past interference in her relationship with Joshua. "Between Janet and the rest of the board, someone was bound to have a way to connect with him."

When she told Janet about A.S. agreeing to compose a brand-new piece for the Hana Trio, her mentor had read the plea in Angie's eyes and hadn't asked any questions. She accepted the good news with delight and promised Angie not to let anyone know she had a part in getting the A.S. commission. The fewer people who knew about A.S.'s identity the better, especially when it came to her connection to him.

"I heard Claudia, the second violin, telling some of the orchestra members that she had a part in finding A.S." Chloe shared this piece of gossip, shaking her head with disdain. "But I don't believe a word she says. She once implied that she had a *thing* with Joshua Bell, but he didn't so much as nod at her when he performed with us."

"You never know..." Angie said with a careless shrug. As ridiculous as Claudia's claim was, she was relieved she wasn't the one drawing the attention.

"No, it's not Claudia," Megan said. "But it really could be any of the musicians."

"I highly doubt that." Angie took a big gulp of her *boricha*. Luckily for her, the barley tea had cooled down to room temperature. "The important thing is that the Hana Trio is going to have the honor to perform A.S.'s new piece. We have to be in top form not to let the Chamber Music Society down. Not to mention what it could do for our reputation. It's make-or-break time, girls."

"Don't worry, Unni," Megan said with a cocky smirk. "We're going to slay it."

Angie and her sisters fist-bumped each other across the table. This was the opportunity of a lifetime, and they had never been more ready. She was so proud of them.

As they finished their lunch, her phone dinged in her purse. Her sisters and she had a no-cell-phone policy during mealtimes, so she just ignored it. Or at least she tried. She couldn't help wondering if the text was from Joshua, and the rest of lunch passed in a bit of a blur.

As soon as she got in her car, Angie dug out her phone from her purse and checked the text.

Grandfather is out of the ICU. He wants you to come. He misses you.

Angie's heart pounded so hard she thought it might burst out of her chest. *He misses you.* Did Joshua miss her, too? She shook her head to dispel the silly thought. She needed to respond to him. Should she ask him how he was doing? Or should she pretend that nothing had happened between them like he seemed to be?

Nah. That might have worked with the kiss, but this was different. They couldn't sweep this under the carpet. Their coffee dates had been fun, but from the way Joshua was behaving, their trips to the café were obviously at an end. Besides being sort of friends with him had been confusing as hell. They needed to discuss this like two adults and clarify whatever they had between them. She typed a quick response.

I'll see you at eight. We can talk after I play for your grandfather.

Angie found Joshua standing in the hospital lobby, waiting for her. When she walked up to him, his eyes roamed her body with such fire that she sucked in a sharp breath. But he blinked and the fire was gone.

"I'll show you to my grandfather's room," he said stiffly.

Without another word, he stepped toward the elevators, so she followed, tugging along her cello. They got off a floor earlier than before and walked down the corridor on the other side of the building.

"This is it," Joshua said, breaking the silence.

"I see. Thank you," she said politely. This was getting ridiculous. Was it going to be this awkward between them from now on? "May I go in?"

"Yes, he's waiting for you." He extended his arm toward the door and she walked past him into the room.

"Halabuji," she said, blinking back tears.

She rushed to the bedside and picked up the patient's hand. The hospital lights accentuated his pallor and his hospital gown hung loosely around his thin figure. He seemed so frail…it broke her heart. Without meaning to, she glanced over her shoulder at Joshua, her eyes full of sympathy.

"Ah, my child. You come to me at last," Mr. Shin said, squeezing her hand. His voice sounded stronger than he looked, and Angie sighed in relief.

"You gave me quite a scare. Please don't do it again," she said firmly, tugging down her eyebrows in an exaggerated frown. "You promised me you'd get better."

"And I'm a man of my word." Some color rose in his cheeks as he chuckled. "When I get my strength back, I'm going to get the old ticker fixed once and for all."

"We decided to go forward with the heart bypass surgery," Joshua explained.

"It's for the best," his grandfather said resolutely.

"And you'll be as good as new." Angie smiled at him despite a flutter of nerves. He was strong. He was going to pull through the open heart surgery. "I've been brushing up on some of the pieces on your list. Let me play for you."

"Nothing would make me happier."

Joshua hurried to his grandfather's side and raised the bed, helping him sit up. After making sure Mr. Shin was comfortable, he pulled a chair close to the bed and sat down heavily. He seemed bone weary.

Although she'd planned on playing another piece, she impulsively decided on Bach's Cello Suite no. 2 in D Minor. It was one of Joshua's favorite pieces, and it also happened to be on his grandfather's list. Angie played, infusing her concern and sympathy into the piece, hoping they would take solace in the music.

His grandfather watched her as though mesmerized, a soft smile on his lips. Joshua closed his eyes, and the tight lines of worry around his eyes and mouth smoothed away. Angie felt her own soul relax and heal as she threw herself into the music. She played the rest of the piece with her eyes closed, and only opened them once the last vibrations of the cello melted into the air.

Joshua clapped and his grandfather held out his

hands to her. She put aside her cello, and clasped them in her own.

"Thank you, my dear."

"My pleasure, as always." She squeezed his hands before releasing them. "Now you really need your rest."

Joshua rose from his seat to walk her out. "I'll be back after I walk Angie to her car."

"No, you won't. You've been here for over an hour. I need a break from looking at your tired mug," his grandfather said gruffly. "Get some rest, my boy. Worrying about you doesn't help me one bit."

When Joshua opened his mouth to argue, Angie put her hand on his arm. "You're going to burn yourself out. Listen to your grandfather. He'll rest easier."

"Smart girl," the patient said with a wink.

Joshua gave her a curt nod, then helped his grandfather get settled before following her out into the hallway. They retraced their steps to the elevators and strode out into the evening air. Angie couldn't stand the uneasy silence that fell between them as they walked to her car. In that instant, she knew what she needed to do.

When they stopped in front of her car, Joshua dug his hands into his pockets and cleared his throat. "Thank you for coming."

"Of course. I have no intention of not keeping my part of our deal." She crossed her arms over her chest, tired of his distant politeness. "Besides, I love playing for your grandfather."

"So...you'll come see him again soon?"

The vulnerable tilt of his head diffused some of her frustration. In a gentler voice, she said, "Yes, I'll visit him twice a week as we agreed."

Huffing out a sigh, Joshua dragged his hand through his hair. "About the other night—"

"It happened," she swiftly interrupted. Then she took in a deep breath for courage. "And... I want it to happen again."

Joshua's eyes snapped to hers, shock and something like hunger crossing his face. "What are you saying?"

This awkward limbo they were in was insufferable. Their agreement bound them together and they had to find a way for whatever they had to work. In order to do that, they had to be honest with themselves and each other. They had to stop fighting their attraction.

"Let me see your phone," she said, holding her palm out.

"Excuse me?" He arched an arrogant eyebrow.

"Your phone, please."

Joshua shrugged his broad shoulders and handed her his phone. She quickly typed something into his map app and returned it to him.

Before he could ask, Angie explained, "That's my address. We need to talk."

"You want me to come over to your place? To-night?"

"Yes and yes." She squared her shoulders and is-sued a challenge. "Will you?"

He studied her with an inscrutable gaze for long

enough to make her want to fidget. Before she succumbed to the urge, he said, "Yes."

She was both relieved and panicked. *Now what?*

Joshua had figured from her address that she didn't live in the most stellar neighborhood, but the rundown facade of her apartment complex made him pause. He circled the block several times before he found street parking. Angie was waiting for him inside when he reached the entrance to the building and opened the door for him.

"I hope it wasn't too difficult to find parking," she said apologetically.

"Not at all." He glanced around the dim, tired lobby and couldn't hold back a frown. He would never have imagined her living in a place like this.

"This way." She led him to the elevators, and pressed the button.

The cramped elevator ride to the third floor took longer than it should've, and Joshua wondered when the elevator was last inspected. It was none of his business but he couldn't help but worry about Angie's living situation. After a short walk down a narrow corridor, she stopped and turned to him.

"This is me," she said, unlocking the door and leading him inside.

Her apartment was small, but it was surprisingly warm and charming. It was her home, and many of his misgivings about her living situation melted away when he saw it.

"Nice place," he said, removing his shoes on the floor mat in front of the door.

"Thank you." She set her cello by a music stand in the corner of the living room. There was pride in her voice when she said, "It's not much but it's mine."

"I assumed you still lived with your father." He didn't want to pry, but he couldn't help but wonder. Even if she'd wanted her own place, why did she choose this neighborhood to live in?

"I had a falling-out with him after my mom died," she said vaguely. She walked toward the kitchen and he followed.

"A falling-out?" he said in a deliberately moderate tone. After she shattered his heart and soul for her precious trust fund, she'd just up and walked away from everything? He fought his confusion and rising anger. Their relationship was in the past. What she chose to do with her life after she left him was none of his business.

"Wine?" she asked, holding up a bottle of red.

"Sure." He picked up the wine opener from the counter and held out his hand. With a shrug, she passed him the bottle. He opened it and poured out two glasses.

She reached for her glass and raised it up. "Cheers."

"Cheers." He tapped his glass against hers, still distracted by what she'd said. Did her falling-out with her father have anything to do with her mother's death? *It wasn't any of his business but he couldn't stop himself from saying,* "I'm sorry about your mother. I remember you were close to her."

"Thank you." Angie circled the rim of her glass with her fingertip. She was quiet for so long that he didn't think she would continue. "It was breast cancer. She fought like a warrior—full of grace and strength—but lost the battle after five years."

It seemed to hurt her to talk about it, so he laid a hand on her shoulder to comfort her. So much had changed since they'd been together, he shouldn't jump to conclusions about her independence from her father.

"Let's go sit," she said with an unsteady smile. She walked out to the living room and sat on one end of the sofa, tucking her legs under her. He took the other end, resting one arm on the back of the couch.

She glanced at him from under her lashes. "I miss our trips to the café."

So did he, but he couldn't go back to pretending that he didn't want her. Memories of their night together refused to be quieted, and he hungered for her even now. "Angie..."

"It almost felt like we were becoming friends," she mused, swirling her wine.

"We can't be friends," he said bluntly. He wanted her to the point of distraction. A platonic relationship with her would be impossible.

He thought he could stop thinking about her by staying away from her but that wasn't the case. Not at all. And distancing himself from her had done nothing to help him compose. He didn't have a single note written for the Hana Trio. It was as though his overwhelming desire for her held his creativity hostage.

Maybe the only way to free it was to let his attraction run its course.

"I don't want us to be friends," she replied with a wry quirk of her lips. Although he was the one who'd said it first, her agreement made his stomach clench with disappointment. "I want you too much for that to be possible."

"Where is this going?" he asked even as his blood rushed below his belt at her bold admission.

"Well, that depends." She took a sip of her wine and licked away a wayward drop from the corner of her mouth. "Do you want me?"

Did he want her? Frustration and desire flooded him. His voice was a near growl when he said, "You know I want you."

"Do you plan on doing something about that?" A sultry smile spread across her face.

This Angie, a sexy-as-hell siren, was the woman he had made love to the other night. The woman he couldn't resist. He hardened his heart and steeled his resolve. "I can't make you any promises."

Her smile faltered but returned full force a split second later. "I have a confession to make. I don't have much time to date, and that night with you was the best sex I've had in a long, long time. Simple as that. The attraction between us is undeniable, and I think we should let it run its course. I don't expect anything beyond that."

"It can only be sex," he said, more to convince himself than her. If he acted on this dangerous attraction, he had to make sure his feelings didn't get involved. He couldn't risk another heartbreak.

"Scorching hot, earth-shattering sex." She raised her arm to the back of the couch and tangled her fingers through his.

He tightened his hold on her hand despite his hesitation. She was telling him everything he wanted to hear, but there was still a chance that she could get hurt… He tipped back his wine and put the glass down on the coffee table. Who did he think he was? Angie was a grown woman who had a right to make her own decisions. It wasn't his responsibility to protect her from himself.

"The best sex, huh?" Shifting on the sofa, Joshua took Angie's glass from her hand and placed it beside his.

"Well, didn't you think so?" she said, lifting her chin.

"Yes." He reached out and tucked a strand of hair behind her ear, and she shivered at his touch. "It was incredible. *You* were incredible."

Her cheeks flushed even as a triumphant smile lit her face. "So what's holding you back?"

"What's holding me back from amazing, uncomplicated sex?" He leaned in until their breath mingled. "Nothing."

He kissed her gently, tasting the fragrant wine lingering in her mouth. Then he traced his lips along her jawline and kissed the sensitive spot behind her ear. As he expected, a shiver ran through her. Yes, he knew her body, but he was more than happy to get reacquainted with it. He lifted her shirt over her head and ran his hands down her torso from the sides of her breasts to her narrow waist. Her curves had grown lusher since college. His greedy fingers dug into her skin, but he forced himself to relax his hold. He wanted to take his time with her tonight.

She fisted her hands into his hair and dragged his lips back to hers. But he drew away after a while and said against her ear, “Slowly. We have time.”

“Slowly?” She stared at him with a slightly glazed look. “You can’t be serious.”

“It’ll be worth it. I promise,” he drawled in a low, seductive voice. She pouted in response.

Joshua rose from the couch and stood just out of her reach. As he began unbuttoning his shirt, Angie’s eyelashes fluttered and her lips parted. Once he was done with all the buttons, he shrugged his shirt off his shoulders and let it drop to the ground.

“Your turn. Take your bra off,” he said in a gravelly voice he hardly recognized.

A provocative smile spread across Angie’s face as she ran the back of her hand down her throat and lower, through the valley between her breasts to her navel. She gathered her hair over one shoulder and reached behind her to unclasp her bra. The breath he’d been holding rushed out in a whoosh when she cast it aside and proudly faced him.

He was shaking with the need to touch her, but he held himself back. He unbuckled his belt at a leisurely pace that belied his desperation, and pushed his pants past his hips. Angie sucked in a breath, as she took in his aching erection still trapped by his boxer briefs. He smiled wolfishly as he kicked away his pants. Making sure her eyes were on him, he reached down and squeezed himself, groaning at the jolt of pleasure.

"Is it my turn?" she asked in a husky voice.

Holding his gaze, she cupped her bare breasts and sucked in a hard breath when her thumbs brushed her hard peaks. She bit her lower lip and tilted her head back as she rolled her nipples between her fingers. *Fuck.* He broke and lunged for her. She planted her hands on his chest and held him off.

"Uh-uh," she said breathlessly. "Slowly. Remember?"

"To hell with slow," Joshua growled, laying her down against the arm of the sofa. He captured her hands above her head and crushed his mouth against hers.

"About damn time." She freed her hands from his grasp and scraped her fingers down his back.

He shuddered against her touch and dipped his head to capture her nipple in his mouth. She moaned and writhed against him, and he sucked her harder. Needing to touch and see all of her, he roughly pulled down her skirt, and her panties soon followed.

"God, you're beautiful," he whispered.

He reverently kissed the inside of her thigh and then let his lips travel upward. He gently opened her up and placed a lingering, openmouthed kiss on her center.

"Joshua," she moaned.

"Yes, Angie?" He licked her with the flat of his tongue.

"Please." She gasped and buried her hands in his hair.

"Please what?" He flicked her nub with his tongue, then pulled her into his mouth. "Is this what you want?"

"Yes. More." Her hips rose off the couch.

"More? Like this?" He pushed her back down and swirled his tongue, easing a finger inside her.

"Oh, God, yes." She was close and it was driving him wild.

He continued tasting her as though she was a decadent dessert, and she buried her fingers in his hair, holding him against her. His tongue matched the speed of his fingers and he didn't relent until she arched her back with a hoarse cry.

Once he covered himself with a condom, he pulled her toward him. She straddled his thighs and lowered herself onto his throbbing cock. He arched his hips off the sofa and thrust deeper so she cradled all of him.

"God, you feel so good," he groaned.

Angie planted her hands on top of his shoulders and increased her speed to a maddening tempo. He was so turned on, he didn't know how long he would last.

"I need you to come for me." He gripped her ass and thrust hard into her, growing desperate as he felt his climax approaching. "Come for me. Please."

Sucking in a sharp breath, she rode him fiercely. As her moaning grew louder, he reached between them to rub his thumb against her swollen clit. They came together with a ragged cry, and Angie sagged limply against him. He cradled her head against his chest and held her close, reluctant to let the moment end.

"That was amazing," Angie murmured, her words slightly slurred. "Let's take a catnap and do it again."

Joshua chuckled and kissed the top of her head. "Anything you want, baby."

Seven

Angie lay warm and satiated beside Joshua as he drew lazy circles on her sweat-slick back. Most evenings, they came to his condo after visiting his grandfather because her bed was too small to fit his tall, broad frame. But the point had been moot until now, because tonight was the first time they actually made it as far as his bed.

Aside from the spectacular sex, there was an added bonus to them being together. Since they weren't trying to hide their attraction from each other, their conversations became easy and comfortable. They sometimes lost track of time and talked late into the night.

But as she grew closer to him, the secret she kept from him weighed heavily on her. She had to tell him why she left him ten years ago. Her excuse that it wouldn't make a difference felt shallow and cowardly now.

She wasn't looking to change what they had between them. A small voice inside her protested, but she shut it out. They might not be in a real relationship but she still owed him the truth. She just hoped she could restore some of the trust he'd lost in her. It hurt her to think that he still believed she had cared more about her trust fund than him. The longer she put it off, the harder it would be for her to tell him, so she jumped in head first.

"There's something you need to know." She raised herself on her elbow and looked into his eyes. "I didn't leave you because I was afraid of my father cutting me off. I didn't give a damn about my trust fund."

His hand froze on her back and his eyebrows rose high on his forehead. "What?"

"I lied to you so that you would let me go." She drew in a shaky breath and the words tumbled out of her. "My mom was diagnosed with cancer, and my father said that if I didn't end things with you, he would never allow me into his house again. I know my mom would've found ways to see me, but the stress of a feud between me and my father would've broken her heart. She needed all her strength to beat the cancer, not to worry over me."

His mouth opened and closed several times before he spoke. "You didn't think I would understand if you told me?"

"I was afraid you would fight for me." A sob broke

free. "If you had so much as asked me to stay, I wouldn't have been able to leave you. I thought the only way you would let me go was to break your heart so completely that you would never think of me again."

"All these years, I believed you left me because money meant more to you than I did." There was so much pain and anger in his voice. Even after a decade.

"You meant *everything* to me." She sat up, holding the sheet against her chest.

"Yet, you still left me," he said with a bitter laugh. He swung his legs off the bed and reached down to pick up his pants. "Do you realize what that did to me?"

"I'm sorry I hurt you." She impatiently wiped her wet cheeks. She didn't want to burden him with her tears "I didn't know what else to do."

"You should have trusted me," he bit out, swinging around to face her.

"I was only eighteen and heartbroken over my mom's diagnosis," she beseeched him to understand. "I realize now that I could have done things differently, but I did what I thought I had to do back then."

Joshua paced the floor, frustration and regret shifting across his face.

"As soon as my mom passed away, I left my father's house," she continued. "He cut me off completely, but I didn't care. I couldn't forgive him for what he did to us."

"What happens if your father finds out about our

current…arrangement?" he asked with a sardonic twist of his lips.

Arrangement. He couldn't even make himself call what they had a relationship. It didn't matter. She hadn't told him the truth to gain something out of it. She told him because he deserved to know.

"Nothing," she said, lifting her chin. She didn't know where their *arrangement* was headed, but she would never allow her father to factor into it again. This was between her and Joshua. "He has no say in what I do with my life anymore."

He stared unblinkingly at her for a long moment then stalked out of the room with a muttered curse.

She clamped her hand over her mouth to stop a sob from escaping. She didn't think telling him the truth would be easy, but she wished Joshua didn't have to hurt. After taking a shuddering breath, she gathered her clothes off the floor and got dressed.

Angie found him in the living room, staring out the window. The city lights twinkled beautifully below but she doubted he saw any of it. He looked so alone standing there with his back toward her. She walked up to him and hugged him from behind.

"I wish…" He sighed and placed his hands over hers. "I wish we could turn back time, so neither of our hearts got broken."

"I'm so sorry." Hot tears streaked down her face and wet the back of his shirt. Joshua stood still, smoothing his thumb over the back of her hand until the floodgates closed.

For the past ten years, a part of her had been tied

up with cold, hard chains that bit into her soul, but those chains finally fell away, allowing her to take a true full breath. But how did Joshua feel? Would he forgive her now that he knew the whole story? And where would that leave them?

"You know what we need right now?" he said, turning around to face her.

"What?" she asked with a tremulous smile.

"Cookies." He grinned boyishly. "We need loads of cookies."

Warmth spooled in her heart and her throat tightened with emotion. He must still be reeling from her confession but he was trying to comfort her. He knew cookies were her ultimate comfort food.

"Let's bake some," he announced.

"I'm sorry." She blinked in surprise. "Are you telling me you bake?"

"No, but I'm very good at following instructions. We'll just look up a recipe online."

"I hope you're not planning to rely on me." She eyed him sideways. "I've never baked before."

"Come on." He grabbed her hand and tugged her toward the kitchen. "It'll be fun."

"If you say so." Images of burnt cookies and a smoke filled condo crowded her head. She could almost hear the wailing of the smoke alarm. "Do you even have ingredients for cookies?"

"I don't have chocolate chips or anything like that, but maybe there's a simple recipe for sugar cookies."

Standing at the kitchen island, they scrolled through the search results with their heads bent over the tablet. Then something caught her eyes and she pointed to the screen. “Look. It says the world’s simplest cookie recipe.”

“That sounds promising,” he murmured, opening up the page. “They’re peanut butter cookies.”

“Ooh, I love peanut butter cookies.” She leaned in for a better look. “Look how short the ingredient list is. You should have everything.”

Joshua rummaged around his kitchen, opening and closing cabinets and drawers. Then he turned to her with a grin. “What do you know? I actually do.”

“Lucky us.” She smiled back at him. His excitement was contagious. “This recipe really is super simple. I think we can do this.”

He brought out his measuring cups and spoons and stared bemusedly at them. Then he held up a quarter-teaspoon measuring spoon. “These look like toys.”

She laughed. It did look like something from a play kitchen in his big hand. “Have you ever used them before?”

“No.”

“Well, you’re the one who suggested this, so let’s get started.” She read through the recipe twice to make sure she understood what she was supposed to do. “Okay. It says to add one and a half cups of flour. And you need to level it.”

“Level it?” He scooped up some flour with the one-cup measuring cup and slid a chopstick over the uneven surface to smooth it out. “Like this?”

“I think so,” she said, watching him repeat the process with the half-cup measuring cup. "We need to do that with all the dry ingredients."

"We? So far, it seems like I'm the only one getting my hands dirty." He already had some flour on the bridge of his nose.

"Not only your hands." She reached across and wiped the flour off his face. "Anyway, I do better giving orders than doing the actual work."

"You're not getting out of this that easily." Joshua reached out and ran his flour-covered hand down the side of her face. "That's better."

"Hey." She tried to wipe the flour off her face but based on his laughter, she apparently only managed to smear it more. "You're going to pay for that."

She grabbed a fistful of flour and threw it at him. He swerved to the side and it mostly missed him, but his hair was dusted with it.

"It's war, then," he said.

When he picked up the entire bag of flour, she ran out of the kitchen with a yelp and planted herself in the middle of the living room.

"You can't throw around flour in the living room," she warned. "You'll ruin all your furniture, not to mention your piano."

"Cheater."

"Being a brilliant strategist does not make one a cheater." She cocked her hip to the side and placed her fist on her waist. "Anyway, I'm really invested in making those cookies now, so stop messing around. Truce?"

"Fine. Truce." He pointed at his eyes and then at her. "But I'll be watching you."

Once they were back in the kitchen, she checked the tablet to see what they needed to do next. "Okay. You keep putting together the dry ingredients, and I'll work on the wet ingredients."

The butter needed to be softened, so she cut it up into small cubes and microwaved it for a few seconds. That probably wasn't the way to do it, but she had to improvise. Then she added the butter and sugar into a mixing bowl and whisked it by hand since Joshua didn't own an electric mixer of any sort. After a few minutes, her arm burned like she had done two minutes of plank.

"Do you need help?" Joshua asked.

He scooped out a bit of the mixture with his finger and licked it off. Angie watched with her mouth open and forgot what they were talking about. With a knowing smile, he leaned in and kissed her with his butter-and-sugar-flavored mouth. She pulled back before they forgot all about the cookies.

"Yes, please." She cleared her throat and handed him the whisk and bowl. She became mesmerized by how amazing his arm looked as he whipped away, but to her disappointment, he made quick work of the creamy mixture. "That looks ready. Now I'm going to add the dry ingredients a little bit at a time."

Her favorite part of the recipe was flattening the scooped dough with a fork to give it the classic crisscross look of a peanut butter cookie. "Ooh, look how fancy these are."

Joshua chuckled and continued scooping out little mounds of cookie dough onto the baking sheets. They worked in cozy silence until all the cookie dough was laid out on the trays and ready to be baked.

"Will you do the honors?" he asked, gesturing at the oven.

"I would love to." Biting her lip with nervous anticipation, she put the first batch of cookies in.

They stood in front of the oven, ready to watch the cookies the entire nine minutes it took to bake them. She leaned her head against him and he wrapped his arm around her waist. Baking with Joshua and enjoying the warmth of the sweet-smelling kitchen felt like the most natural thing to do. She sighed happily.

Then she caught herself. Cute domestic situations weren't part of their arrangement. Just because he knew the truth about their breakup didn't mean that he suddenly wanted a real relationship with her. She couldn't let herself get used to moments like this—moments when it felt as though she and Joshua belonged together. She stepped away from him and began wiping down the counters. But he came up behind her and wrapped his arms around her.

"Hey, what's wrong?" His hot breath tickled her ear and an involuntary shiver ran down her spine.

"Nothing. I wanted to help clean up this mess before I left," she said lightly, hoping he would buy her act. Or maybe a part of her hoped that he would ask her to stay the night. Now that she'd confessed, the proverbial ball was in his court.

"Don't worry about it. Leaving the mess behind is

one of the perks of being a guest." He gave her a swift peck on the cheek then gathered up the used bowls and utensils to place in the sink. "I'm just going to stick these in the dishwasher after you leave."

She squashed the sting of disappointment and forced herself to smile. "I think the cookies are ready."

Joshua hurried to the oven and took out the cookies, and placed another sheet of cookie dough inside. The cookies looked and smelled perfect. But when he reached out for one, Angie slapped his hand away.

"We need to let it sit for five minutes."

"Bossy," he said, rubbing his hand.

In the end, they only managed to wait for three minutes before they each grabbed a cookie off the baking sheet.

"Mmm," they moaned in unison and laughed.

The warm, soft cookie was just the right amount of sweet, salty and nutty. In her opinion, it was even better than the ones she got at cafés. A corner of her heart still felt hollow but the sugar rush was helping her mood. She was content with her relationship with Joshua. It didn't have to mean something or last forever. She was happy with the now.

When all the batches were done, Angie filled up a good-sized plastic container with her half of the cookies. She wouldn't be spending the night with Joshua, but she had her cookies to keep her company.

Eight

Angie leaned back in her tub and sank her head under water. She was done with practices for the day and had time for a leisurely soak. But she kept her hands out of the hot water, so they wouldn't get pruney and desensitize her fingertips.

When most of the bubbles fizzed out and the water turned lukewarm, she unplugged the tub and stepped out of it. She toweled herself off, thinking about her date with Joshua in a couple of hours. *A date.* She pursed her lips as she cinched the belt of her bathrobe. Other than their trips to the café before they…well… before, they had never been on a date. They met. They had sex. They talked—they always talked. But that was it. They didn't go out and do things that real couples did. Like go on dates.

She walked listlessly to her room and fell back on her bed. She shouldn't read too much into it. It was just a date. It probably had nothing to do with her confession.

The cookies from that night were long gone but her disappointment that he didn't invite her to stay lingered. She didn't know what she'd expected to happen after she told him the truth but *nothing* wasn't it. Maybe this date meant…*something*. She flopped onto her stomach and buried her face in her pillow.

He was cryptic about the plan, saying something about a dinner and a concert. She should have asked him what kind of concert it was—the ripped jeans kind or the formal dress kind or something in between. Grabbing her phone from her nightstand, she shot him a quick text.

What's the dress code for this mystery dinner and concert?

She put her phone back down and sat up in bed. It was time to face the truth. She was no longer content with their *arrangement*. She wanted more. It was foolish, especially since Joshua didn't want anything more—he'd made that clear from the beginning—but she couldn't stop herself from caring about him and wishing that he could come to care about her, too.

That didn't mean she was willing to do anything about it. Angie sighed and got to her feet. She opened her closet door and stared at her many dresses. Most of them were for performances; they had full skirts with room to cradle her cello between her legs. She could also wear them on the rare occasions that she went to watch someone else play. She sometimes wished she had dresses that hugged her curves—something sexy and flirty. But she couldn't buy dresses for fun on her budget.

Her intercom rang, which meant that someone was outside. A deliveryman? *Odd.* She hadn't ordered anything recently.

"Who is it?" she asked, picking up the receiver.

"I have a package for Angie Han," a man answered.

Hmm. "Okay. Come on up."

The box was big—the size of a sheet cake but taller. She thanked the delivery guy and closed the door with her butt, juggling the box in her arms. She plopped it down on the sofa and took off the card attached to it.

I want you to wear this so I can peel it off you tonight.
Joshua

Angie couldn't stop the excitement that coursed through her. A gift like this had to mean something, didn't it? Or maybe he just didn't want his date to look like a frumpy matron. It didn't matter. It was a gift and she was going to enjoy it.

She opened the box with trembling hands and gasped with delight. Apparently he was taking her to a formal concert tonight. She held the gold-sequined, strapless dress against herself and rushed to the mirror hanging on her closet door. The floor-length mermaid gown was something she could never wear to one of her performances. It was absolutely impractical and ridiculously expensive—based on the designer label—but she didn't care. She loved it.

Stripping off her T-shirt and shorts, Angie slipped on the gown and zipped up the low back. It fit her like a glove. *Wow.* Were those really her curves? She was far from a pin up, but damn… She had some va-va-va-voom in her. After twisting around in front of the mirror for ages, she reluctantly stepped out of the dress. She didn't want to mess it up while she did her makeup and hair.

She painted on dramatic cat's-eye makeup and pouty red lips to complete her bombshell look. She didn't exactly look like a different person, but she definitely was a different version of herself. Someone bold and adventurous.

She was ready five minutes before Joshua arrived. With her heart beating faster than usual, Angie opened the door for him and froze. Joshua was wearing a classic tuxedo that emphasized his broad shoulders and narrow waist. He looked so gorgeous that she forgot to breathe for a second. But her favorite part was his expression—eyebrows high, eyes wide and mouth hanging open. She either looked stunningly hideous or beautiful enough to make him speechless.

"Hello, handsome," she said, finally finding her voice.

Fire lit Joshua's eyes as they roamed her body from top to bottom and back again. "Let's stay in tonight."

She tilted her head back and laughed huskily. "Not a chance. You promised me dinner and a show."

"After that," he said in a low growl, "I'm going to get you naked."

Her breath quickened and lust flared inside her. "Promise?"

"Let's go," he said.

She raised her eyebrows at his brusque tone.

"We need to leave before I bend you over that sofa and take you from behind."

"Oh," she breathed.

She quickly stepped out and locked her door. Despite her body's protestations, sex would have to wait until after their date. She was dying to know what he had in store for her tonight.

Luckily for her stiletto-clad feet, Joshua had found parking close to her building. Once they were settled in and on their way, Angie couldn't hold back her curiosity.

"So where exactly are we going?" She turned in her seat to face him.

"You'll see when we get there." He shot her a playful grin, then returned his eyes to the road.

"Why are you being so secretive?" She lightly socked his arm.

"Hey," he said, rubbing his arm. "No abusing the driver."

"Just tell me," she pleaded. "Please."

"You used to love surprises. What happened?"

"I still love surprises," she said. "So tell me where we're going so I can be surprised."

"Nice try." Joshua chuckled, shaking his head. "But you'll find out soon. It's not too far."

She slumped back in her seat with a huff. Then she sat up and leaned forward to look through the windshield. They were headed downtown. That narrowed the possibilities a bit.

"Wait. We're going to L.A. Live?" She furrowed her brows. L.A. Live was an outdoor mall on steroids with hip night clubs, restaurants and…a bowling alley. "We're not dressed like this to play glow-in-the-dark bowling, are we?"

"We sure are," he deadpanned. "I thought you'd get a kick out of it."

"If you make me bowl and I hurt my hand, I'm telling your grandfather."

He finally turned onto a smaller street and pulled into a parking structure across from the Staples Center. After handing the keys to the valet, he came around to her side and held out his arm. "Shall we?"

Taking his arm, she grinned triumphantly at him. "So the concert is at the Staples Center?"

Joshua smiled blithely in response and led her to the building's elevator.

"Why are we getting on the elevator here?" she asked. "The Staples Center is across the street."

"You'll see." Joshua pressed the button for the top deck.

The elevator doors opened to reveal throngs of people standing around red, orange, green and blue cocktail tables below crisscrossed string lights. Geometrically-shaped topiaries dotted the whimsically decorated outdoor space, which led to the biggest event tent she had ever seen. Accent lights splashed against its entrance.

"Okay. I'm definitely surprised," she said. "Where are we?"

"This is the Children's Hospital's charity gala," Joshua said a little sheepishly. "I didn't really mean for it to be a surprise, but you were so adorably curious, I couldn't help teasing you. I hope you're not disappointed."

"Why would I be disappointed? You're obviously here as a donor." She leaned in close and said, "Frankly, I'm a little smitten with you now. Helping those children is such an amazing cause."

He scratched the back of his head and the tips of his ears turned pink. "I'm just doing what I can."

"And so modest," she teased.

Joshua led them down the red carpet with a possessive hand on her back, and they posed for the photographers. She felt a little like a star at a movie premiere but the night's excitement was about raising funds for sick children, not the latest blockbuster. She pushed aside the prickle of unease that her sisters might see these pictures—it wasn't like they read through the society pages.

When a server passed with a tray of champagne, she plucked off two flutes. "Here. Let's toast. To the children."

"To the children." He clinked his glass against hers and brought it to his lips.

After drinks and hors d'oeuvres, they were ushered inside the tent. Angie gasped. It was lit up in vibrant purple, and giant versions of the colorful Children's Hospital logo were stamped on the ceiling. The logo reminded her of both a butterfly and a flower, filled with hope and spirit.

They sat down at a table occupied by two older couples, who smiled warmly at them. The server came around to offer them wine, and she chose the white to go along with her scallop entrée.

"It's nice to be a guest at one of these events," she whispered, taking a sip of her chardonnay. "I feel so pampered."

Joshua chuckled. "You deserve it. And rather than performing yourself, you'll get to watch Katy Perry perform."

"Shut the front door." She slapped Joshua's arm. "Katy Perry is singing tonight?"

"Don't believe me? Read the program."

Angie grabbed her program and scanned through it. Her face split into a huge grin when she looked up. "This is so much fun."

"I'm glad you approve." Joshua smiled and pressed a sweet kiss on her lips.

Her heart stuttered, and her breath left her on a soft whoosh. Truth be told, every moment she spent with Joshua was special to her, and she was dangerously close to losing her heart to him once more.

Joshua pulled Angie tighter against him in bed. Her obvious delight at the gala had been contagious, and he had enjoyed the evening. But if he'd had his way, he would have left early and brought her home sooner.

The dress had looked spectacular on her, and he'd steadily lost his mind, wanting to tear it off her. Finally getting her naked had been well worth the wait, though. They were desperate and hungry as they made love, and now they lay spent in each other's arms.

He placed a lingering kiss on her bare shoulder, and she snuggled closer to him. Having her in his arms and in his life felt…right. He couldn't put it any other way. Even when he'd found music again, he couldn't free himself from the piercing discontent that haunted him. With Angie back beside him—and knowing the real reason she'd left him—he felt as though he'd been mended. But she wouldn't stay by his side for long. Not when he couldn't love her like she deserved. Still, his arms tightened around her. She was his for now, and he was going to cherish every moment of it.

Angie pecked him on the lips and untangled herself from him.

"What are you doing?" he asked, pulling her back into his arms.

"It's getting late." She pushed her hands against his chest but he didn't give an inch. "I should head home."

"Stay," he said simply.

He was the one who had insisted on a purely physical relationship but that wasn't enough anymore. He wanted her to need him. He wanted her to trust him. *How about you? Will you be able to trust her? To need her?* He selfishly pushed aside those questions.

She grew still in his arms then slowly raised her eyes to meet his. "You want me to stay?"

"I do."

"You made it clear that a real relationship was out of the question. It'll be the best for both of us to keep things as simple as possible."

"To hell with simple." What was he doing? He must be out of his mind.

"Is this because I told you the truth about why I left you?" she asked quietly, something like hope flaring in her eyes.

"No. Yes. I don't know." He blew out a long breath and tried again. "All I know is I'm not satisfied with just having your body. I want to spend time with you and laugh with you. I want to wake up with you in my arms. Even if it's only for a short while, I want to *be* with you."

"I want those things, too," she said in a whisper.

"I..." He swallowed with difficulty. "I still can't make you any promises—"

"And I'm not asking for any." She lifted her chin but couldn't stop one corner of her lips from wobbling for a second. "I just don't want either of us to get hurt."

His chest clenched with fear and he felt a moment of panic. But wouldn't they be safe from heartbreak as long as they didn't fall in love? He reached out and cupped her cheek. "Let's take things slowly—day by day. Our hearts were broken when we were young because we expected a lifetime with each other. As long as we don't give into such unrealistic expectations, neither of us will get hurt."

He thought he caught a glimpse of bleakness in her eyes, but it was gone when she blinked. "You're right. We'll go into this with our eyes wide open and our hearts safely locked away."

He nodded vigorously to dislodge the sense of loss her words wrought inside him. He leaned toward her and nudged her nose with his. "Does that mean you'll stay the night?"

"Yes, I'll stay."

He held her close as relief and happiness rushed through him. Angie was so quiet for a while he thought she'd fallen asleep.

"I've been meaning to ask," she said hesitantly. "Why do you compose in secret?"

He paused to consider how much he should share with her. She would beat herself up if she found out he couldn't compose for years after she left him. And he didn't want to worry her by telling her about the threat Nathan Whitley posed.

"I don't want my father to worry that I might turn my back on Riddle to pursue music full-time," he offered her a truncated explanation.

"Is that what you want? To compose full-time?"

"No. Riddle means too much to me. Besides, I've been doing this for years now. I know I could successfully run Riddle *and* compose."

"I'm glad," she said. After a pause, she came up on one elbow. "By the way, how is your composition going? When do I get to see it?"

It was the question he dreaded. He was still without a single note after crumpling numerous false starts. But now that his conflicted emotions were becoming untangled, maybe he would be able to compose again.

Even so, he couldn't keep it from her any longer. The Hana Trio and the Chamber Music Society were counting on him, and she deserved to know his lack of progress.

"I have nothing to show you," he said.

"What do you mean you have nothing? Are you not ready to share it with me? Because I would totally understand."

"No, I mean I haven't written a single note." He sighed. "I'm blocked."

Angie propped herself up on her elbow and the sheet slipped down to reveal her creamy breasts. He was immediately distracted and reached out to cup one of them. She slapped his hand away.

"Focus, Joshua. The season is opening in less than two months. That means you have a month at most to finish the piece. My sisters and I need some time to practice, too."

Instead of filling his hand with her glorious flesh, he raked it through his hair. "I know all that. But I can't help it. I'm still blocked."

She swung her feet down to the floor and stood, picking his shirt up off the floor and shrugging into it. She haphazardly buttoned it and tugged his hand. "Get up. I'll help you through this."

"I don't think I'll be able to compose any better with you distracting me. You don't know how sexy you are in that shirt." He didn't budge from his prone position. "Come back to bed, baby."

"All you need is a little inspiration. Once you get started, everything will flow smoothly."

When she pulled harder, putting her back into it, Joshua got out of bed and slipped on his pants. "I'm up. Now what?"

"We brew some coffee and sit at the piano." She headed straight to the kitchen.

"And stare blankly at the keys," he added morosely as he joined her. After grabbing a couple mugs from the cupboard, he started the coffee. "Just so you know, I've tried that already."

"You need to psyche yourself up."

"Psyche myself up?"

"Yeah. When I get stuck on a phrase, I can't get past it without making the same mistake over and over again. The longer that goes on, the more stuck I become. Sometimes, starting a few measures back and playing at a ridiculously fast pace helps me spit out the phrase."

"Interesting." He nodded but couldn't hide his skepticism.

Angie rolled her eyes. "Just trust me. It's all about not overthinking things."

When the coffee was ready, she filled the mugs and carried them out to the living room. She handed him his cup when he came to stand next to her. After a few sips, she waved her hand toward the piano.

"Sit," she ordered.

He put down his mug on a side table and sat at the piano. "I'm sitting. Now what?"

"When you think about the Hana Trio, what's the first word that comes to mind?"

"Fluid," he said without hesitation. Their unified

sound reminded him of a calm, spring river—the water flowing freely without obstruction.

"Don't think too hard on this. How best can you translate that into music?"

He imagined the flowing river and played a single strain on the piano with his right hand. His heart thumped. He used his left hand to add layers and played the strain again.

"That sounds amazing," Angie whispered, her eyes wide. "Run with it, Joshua."

And he did. The sky was clear and blue above the river and the dense forest surrounding it was teeming with life. He heard the violin, cello and viola painting the picture of this river in the depth of a secluded forest. He felt the beginnings of the string trio take form in his mind.

He grabbed a blank piece of music paper from the top of the piano and scribbled notes onto it with a stubby pencil. He alternately wrote and played until he had pages of music spilling over the piano.

A soft sigh brought him out of his frenzied composition. Angie was sitting quietly on the sofa, watching him with a tender light in her eyes.

"Angie… I'm sorry. I got carried away." He extended his arms over his head and stretched his back. "How long have I been inadvertently ignoring you?"

She turned her head to read the wall clock behind her. "Oh, it's only been about an hour."

"You must be tired." He pushed the piano bench back. "Let's go to bed."

"I'm a big girl. I can tuck myself in." She walked up

to him and placed a hand on his shoulder to stop him from getting up. "You're not tired at all. I know how you work for hours on end when something grips you."

Even as they spoke, more notes danced in his mind and he was eager to jot them down. "Thank you. I'll join you in a bit."

She placed a lingering kiss on his lips and turned away before he had a chance to tug her down beside him. He watched his muse walk away clad only in his shirt, her shapely legs bare for his perusal. He almost chased after her, but he held himself back. His music demanded his full attention now.

Nine

It was just Angie and Edward Shin this evening at the Malibu wellness resort. Joshua was held up in a meeting, so she'd decided to stay a bit longer after she played for his grandfather.

"Are you nervous about the surgery?" she asked, placing a hand on his arm.

"Not nervous. Just impatient to get it over with." He sighed wearily. "I'm tired of this place—and don't get me started about the hospital. If it wasn't for your visits, I'll probably fly the coop."

"Hang in there for a bit longer. Your surgery is only a few days away. Then you'll be able to go home."

"Thank you, my dear." He patted her hand. "You're an angel."

She smiled warmly at him. She'd grown so fond of the kind, spirited man.

"I haven't seen Joshua this happy in such a long time," he said, watching her closely.

"Oh?" The sudden change in topic froze her smile on her face.

"You're good for him."

"Well, you know what they say. Music is chicken soup for the soul," she blabbered.

"I'm sure your music helps, too," he said knowingly.

"Halabuji, I'm not sure what you're implying, but Joshua and I are just friends."

"My child, I may be old and sick, but I'm not blind. I see the way you look at each other." He chuckled. "And I know my boy. He's head over heels in love with you."

Angie laughed nervously, which turned into a hiccup. *Joshua. In love with me.* Her heart curled into itself, fighting against the hope that threatened to bloom inside.

"And I think that you're a hopeless romantic," she said affectionately. Standing from her seat, she leaned down to kiss his cheek. "I should leave you to rest."

She spent the entire drive home trying not to think about what her charming patient had said. Then she showered and dried her hair, not thinking about what he'd said. And when the thought *What if?* bubbled up in her mind, she popped it without mercy.

If she considered the possibility that Joshua might love her even a little, then she would have to face her own growing feelings for him. Angie cherished every moment she spent with him. Every smile and every touch made her heart swell with…*like*? Her instinct for self-preservation brought her thoughts to a screeching halt. She couldn't do this.

They had already discussed where the relationship was heading, and commitment wasn't part of the plan after what had happened between them before. How had Joshua put it? *Our hearts were broken when we were young because we expected a lifetime with each other. As long as we don't give into such unrealistic expectations, neither of us will get hurt.* She swallowed the emotion rising up in her throat.

Tea. She needed some tea. What good would it do to wonder about what happened next? When either of them decided to end things, that would be that. And everything would be fine because *unrealistic expectations* like love and forever weren't part of the equation, right? Hot water splashed on the counter as she poured some into her mug. Her hands weren't quite steady.

Grabbing her cup, she settled down on the couch and reached for the remote control. She scrolled through the Trending Now titles on her streaming service without much interest when her phone rang. It was Joshua.

"Hi," she said breathlessly. *No, you don't sound lovesick at all.* "Are you done with your meeting?"

"Yes, I just got home." Silence stretched on a moment too long. "I miss you."

Her hand tightened around the phone and her blood pounded loudly in her ears. Even if it wasn't forever, their relationship was real. And it was perfectly natural for them to miss each other.

"I miss you, too." Inexplicable tears prickled behind her eyes.

"Come over," he said, sexy and demanding.

"I can't." Her emotions were too close to the surface. If she made love to him tonight, she might do or say something she would regret. "I have an early rehearsal tomorrow."

"Then can I keep you on the phone a little longer?"

Why was he making this so hard? Despite her best intentions, her heart turned into mush. "Of course. I'd love to keep you company."

"I wrote some more last night," he said. "Do you want to hear it?"

"Absolutely." Her stomach fluttered with excitement.

She heard him pull out his piano bench. "I'm going to put you on speaker now."

Then he played a lovely strain for her. She could almost see the music dance in her mind's eye. It was fanciful, yet vulnerable. His talent took her breath away.

"That's exquisite," she said softly.

"Thank you." He sounded a bit embarrassed by her praise, and it was adorable. "But I'm not too sure about the next phrase."

"Do you think it'll help if you heard it on the cello?" she said, eager to help.

"That would be fantastic."

She put her phone on speaker and placed it on her

music stand to take out her instrument. When she was ready, she said, "Play it for me again."

He did, and she mimicked him on the cello.

"Huh." He sounded pleasantly surprised. "How about this part?"

He played a slightly different phrase, and she repeated it. Soon they got into a rhythm where he played a phrase of music on the piano and she played it back on her cello. It was exhilarating to witness his creative process and be a part of it.

"I might need to use you for every composition from now on," he finally said.

Angie's heart clenched. He said that as though they had a future together. She steadied her breathing and said lightly, "Well, I better start charging you for it."

He laughed and she felt it down to her toes. Then neither of them spoke for a moment.

"Are you sure you can't come over?"

"Joshua," she said sternly.

"Yes?"

"It's almost midnight." She didn't know how much longer her willpower would last when all she wanted was to run to him.

"I want you, Angie," he said in near growl, turning her knees into Jell-O.

"Stop tempting me." She meant to sound firm but it came out as a plea.

"I can come over to your place," he persisted.

"And what? Sleep on the sofa? You know we can't fit on my twin-size bed together."

"We'll curl up real tight." His voice grew low and seductive.

"I want you, too," she hardened her resolve, "but I have to wait until tomorrow night to have you, and so do you."

"I'll be up all night thinking about you."

Her heart lurched and butterflies took flight in her stomach. How did he expect her not to fall in love with him when he acted like this? Anger suddenly stirred inside her. It wasn't fair.

"Why don't you try some warm milk?" she said with saccharine sweetness.

"That's cold," he grumbled.

She had to laugh at that. But before he could deplete her willpower, she said, "Good night."

"Good night, Angie," he finally relented. "I'll see you in my dreams."

Joshua stood in front of his full-length mirror and adjusted his tie. As he'd predicted, Angie had haunted his dreams all night. When he woke up this morning, his eyes burned and his head felt heavy, but he was happy because he was going to see her tonight. She spent several nights a week at his place, but that wasn't enough. He wanted her in his bed every night. It felt wrong to wake up alone.

He callously swept away the voice that told him he was wandering too close to the flames. This wasn't love. Yes, he cared about her and burned for her, but it wasn't the all-consuming thing that they'd once shared. It could never be that. They already had everything they needed for a satisfying relationship—affection, passion, respect. Love was an unnecessary risk. Because in the end, she'd left him even though she loved him. He wouldn't gamble his heart and music on something that had no guarantee. Not again.

But how long would he be able to keep her without a commitment? A year? Two years? He was the one who said expecting a lifetime together was unrealistic. He pushed his door open with more force than necessary and headed for his car.

The reminder that their relationship couldn't last twisted him up. He brooded over the thought as he made his daily commute. He didn't have to lose her just because he couldn't promise her love and forever. What they had could be enough. Doubt and restlessness were clawing at his chest by the time he arrived at his office.

"Good morning, Joshua. Would you like some coffee?" Janice said cheerily.

He grunted noncommittally.

"I'm going to take that as a yes."

He slung his jacket on the coatrack and dropped heavily into his chair. This was ridiculous. He was working himself up for no good reason. Things were going well. He was seeing her tonight. But tonight seemed too long of a wait. He needed to see her sooner and assure himself that everything was fine. After checking his watch to make sure he wasn't disrupting her rehearsal, he texted her.

I want to take you to lunch.

To his relief, he saw ellipses appear on his messaging app right away.

You couldn't wait till tonight? J

No, as a matter of fact, I couldn't.

This time there was a longish pause before she responded.

Where do you want to meet?

Are you okay coming downtown?

I'm fine with that.

They agreed to meet at a seafood restaurant near his work—he glanced at the clock—in about three hours. Satisfied with the arrangement, he was finally able to concentrate on the work piled on his desk. His plans for Riddle's growth were ambitious and aggressive. He usually worked twelve-hour days to meet the demands of his job but he'd fallen a bit behind since Halabuji's heart attack. He couldn't afford to let his personal life distract him from his work.

He was making good progress when his phone rang, breaking his concentration.

"Yes, Janice?" he said impatiently while he finished typing out an email.

"Clarice Wong is here to see you."

His hands paused over his keyboard. Why was the chairperson of the board of directors here to see him?

"Please send her in." He went around his desk to greet his guest.

"I'm sorry for showing up unannounced." She shook his hand firmly. "But I had a meeting nearby and thought I'd drop in to see if you had a minute."

"I'm glad you did." He motioned for her to take a seat on the couch and sat down across from her.

"How's your grandfather?" she asked with genuine concern. She was a close family friend.

"He's a fighter," Joshua said. "He'll come back stronger than ever."

"I'm sure he will." The softness in her expression disappeared as she got down to business. "I trust the Nexus contract is progressing smoothly."

"Without a hitch," he said with confidence. "Is there reason for concern?"

"Whitley." Clarice blew out a frustrated breath. "He's been implying that you're distracted with your grandfather's illness and that Nexus might not be renewing their contract with Riddle at the end of the year."

"That's funny. A few days ago, the COO of Nexus assured me that she had every intention of renewing Nexus's contract with Riddle." Joshua crossed his legs and leaned back on the sofa. "I hope no one on the board is buying Whitley's bullshit. Other than Richard Benson and Scott Grey, that is."

"Benson is apparently a business school buddy of

his but Grey is still on the fence. The problem is there are a few others that are on the fence," she said. "The Nexus contract aside, Whitley's best offense is that you're young and unproven."

"My grandfather started Riddle when he was my age." His voice grew cold with anger. "And my track record as vice president of operations more than proves my competence."

"But you can't afford to make any mistakes at this point. Remember Whitley is a formidable opponent."

"Thank you for your advice," he said sincerely. "I assure you there won't be any mistakes."

By the time Clarice left, he was late for lunch. He sprinted the two blocks to the restaurant and when he reached Angie's table, he was out of breath. He dropped a kiss on her lips and sat across from her. "I'm sorry I'm late. A meeting took longer than I expected."

"Don't worry about it." Her smile was open and warm, and Joshua's heart skipped a beat. "I was just looking over the menu. It always takes me forever to make my decision."

"That's good." He didn't bother picking up his menu. "I always get the same thing here."

Lunch service was quick and efficient. His lobster roll and her grilled salmon were ready within minutes.

"How was practice?" he asked, his eyes roaming her beautiful face. Just being with her eased some of the tension from his meeting with Clarice.

"Megan seemed a little distracted today. It took us a

while to come together," she answered between bites. "We're eager to start practicing A.S.'s new piece."

"I think he's close to finishing." The tables were pretty close together, so he had to watch his words. "With his muse's help, he should be able to wrap it up this weekend."

"I can't wait to get my hands on it. The Chamber Music Society launched its publicity campaign for the upcoming season—highlighting the premiere of A.S.'s new work. They're already getting so much positive feedback."

"I'm glad it's helping them," he said with a smile, but his chest tightened with worry.

The heightened publicity was going to fuel the search for A.S.'s true identity. It happened every time a new piece premiered or a record launched, but the stakes were too high this time. It would be a disaster if his identity as A.S. was revealed so close to the CEO appointment. Like Clarice said, he couldn't afford any mistakes.

"The salmon is great," Angie said, drawing him out of his dark thoughts. "Here, have some. I'll trade you for your fries."

She reached across the table to place a perfectly grilled piece of salmon on the corner of his plate, and grabbed some fries while she was at it. For some reason, the simple act of eating off each other's plates made the uncertainty gnawing at him disappear. He was on solid ground again. There was a familiarity and intimacy to it that marked them as a real couple. He wasn't going to lose her.

* * *

It was Saturday morning and Angie was fast asleep. She'd gone to bed around two o'clock, but having her near had centered Joshua as he stayed up all night to finish the string trio. It was a fine piece but it didn't feel like the right one for the Hana Trio—for Angie. He wanted to create something truly unique and moving for her.

But maybe he wouldn't be happy with anything he wrote for her. Nothing might ever be good enough for her in his mind. *Why was that?* He ignored the voice in his head. Angie played with soul and her unique sound deserved something equally unique. That was all.

He stood from his seat and stretched, twisting this way and that with his arms raised over his head. He sighed in relief as some of the tension left his stiff neck, back and shoulders. Careful not to wake up Angie, he tiptoed to the kitchen and got the coffee going. Then he rummaged around his fridge and gathered the ingredients for a cheese omelet. It was close to nine. She would be hungry when she woke up.

He cracked the eggs into a bowl and briskly beat them with a couple tablespoons of ice water to make the omelet extra fluffy. Once the pan was hot, he poured in the mixture and carefully folded the eggs with a fork then added the cheese near the end. When the food ready, he arranged the plates on the tray and went to his bedroom.

Angie's shiny black hair was fanned out on the white sheets, and her milky shoulder peeked out from under the covers. She was sleeping on her side with her hands softly curled in front of her face. Her beauty made his heart clench and emotion clog his throat. Belatedly remembering to breathe, Joshua set their breakfast on top of the dresser and gingerly climbed into bed beside her.

He leaned down and kissed her shoulder. Her vanilla scent was sweet and welcoming, and the feel of her warm, smooth skin made desire engulf him. Her eyelids fluttered open and she glanced over her shoulder with a sleepy smile.

"Good morning," she murmured.

And because he couldn't help himself, he turned her to face him and kissed her deeply. With a little whimper, she pressed herself to him as she grasped the nape of his neck and kissed him back. He barely held himself in check and slowed down the kiss. With one last featherlight press of his lips, he drew away.

"Good morning," he said in a husky voice. Her lips, plump and red from kissing, formed a hint of a pout, and she tried to pull him back to her. He chuckled and stood up. "Hold that thought."

When he carried the tray over to the bed, Angie sat up, holding the covers against her perfect breasts. "You made me breakfast in bed?" Surprise and happiness colored her voice.

"I hope you like cheese omelets."

"Ooh, that sounds delicious." Tucking the sheets under her arms, she scooted back against the headrest to make room for the tray. He carefully positioned the food in front of her. "But we're finishing what we started after we eat."

"I'll try to keep that in mind." He swept his gaze over her body, not bothering to disguise the desire in his eyes.

Turning a lovely shade of pink, she dug into her omelet, twirling her fork to wrap the strings of melted cheese around it. As she took a bite and chewed, her eyes widened. "Oh, my goodness. This is delicious."

"You don't need to sound so surprised," he teased, sitting down on the edge of the bed beside her.

"I just never knew you were such an amazing cook," she said, taking another bite.

"I can only cook a handful of dishes." He laughed, ridiculously pleased that she was enjoying the omelet. "But I'm glad you like it."

"Why aren't you eating?" She blew on her mug before taking a sip of her coffee.

He'd been pushing around a piece of his omelet, and he put down his fork. "I finished it."

"What?" She put the tray on the other side of bed and enveloped him in a bear hug. "Congratulations, Joshua."

"Thank you," he said into her hair, his arms tightening around her. Finishing a new piece of music had never been more rewarding.

She pushed at his shoulders and he loosened his arms to let her back away a few inches. "Can I see it?"

He tugged her back into his arms, and buried his face in the crook of her neck. "In a minute."

Angie understood what he needed and burrowed

against him, the sheet pooling around her waist. It had been a fight, but with her help, he'd finished the string trio, and at last, she was going to perform his music. They took the long way around, but they finally got here. He dismissed his prior misgivings that the piece wasn't right for her. He would never feel that anything was perfect enough for her.

He allowed contentment, sweety and heady, to flow through him. He didn't need any guarantees about the future. She was in his arms now. That was enough. They were enough.

Ten

Angie checked her phone for the umpteenth time, and sighed forlornly.

"My dear, is everything okay?" Janet asked, taking off her reading glasses. She had been reading the sheet music for A.S.'s string trio. Angie had brought it to her office today.

"Mmm-hmm. Everything's fine. I'm just a little distracted."

Mr. Shin was in surgery right now, and Joshua had promised to update her with any news. She didn't know if the surgery was supposed to last this long. More than anything, she wished she could be by his side, providing her support and comfort. But he was with his parents now, as he should be. They would support each other.

"Does it have anything to do with your…composer friend?"

"No, no. It's nothing like that," Angie said in a rush.

This was the first time her mentor had alluded to her relationship to A.S. Janet never pried into how she knew the composer and even managed to keep Angie's name out when she informed Timothy about the commission for the string trio. Angie owed her an explanation but it wasn't her secret to share.

"Janet, I wish… I'm…" What could she say? "I'm sorry."

"Don't be. I know you have your reasons." Her words held no judgment. "But I'm here for you if you ever need anything. Don't forget."

"I won't. Thank you for understanding," Angie said, blinking back tears. She sniffed and shook her head to clear it. "So what do you think? Does A.S.'s new work live up to your expectations?"

"This is simply marvelous. He has to be one of the most talented composers of our generation," Janet gushed, hugging the music to her chest. Recovering her composure, she slipped the pages back into the folder. "I can't wait to hear you girls play it."

"We start rehearsals tomorrow." Angie's heart pounded loudly in her ears. She was both thrilled and anxious. What if she couldn't do Joshua's music justice?

"Are you nervous?" Her mentor knew her well.

"Very," Angie admitted.

"Your playing is reaching new heights. A.S. should

be honored to have you and your sisters premiere his piece."

"And I think you may be a bit partial to the trio," Angie said with a warm smile.

"That doesn't make me wrong."

"Thank you, Janet." She stood from her seat and went around the desk to hug her friend. "Your faith in me fills me with courage. I'll make you proud."

"I know you will." Janet squeezed her tight and patted her back. "You always do."

"I'm going to let you get back to work. I know you're busy preparing for the maestro's circle event next week."

"Yes, it's for our biggest donors. I have to give a rousing speech to make them itch to write very generous checks." Janet laughed about the part of the job that was most difficult for her. Asking people to hand out hard-earned money was never easy even when it was for a good cause. "Are you and your sisters preparing for the performance?"

"We're practicing Bach's Goldberg Variations." They had sounded pretty great at their rehearsal this morning. She remembered the sense of accomplishment that had filled her. She loved being a musician. "We'll warm up the crowd for you."

"Good, good. And I think the excitement over our collaboration with A.S. will make for an exceptional evening."

"I'm glad." Angie smiled, happy to see how valuable Joshua's help was to the Chamber Music Society. "I'll see you then."

Angie rolled her cello case out, greeting some of her fellow musicians on her way to the parking lot. There was a palpable energy and excitement in the air. They were finally resuming live performances. This season was going to be remarkable. She could feel it.

Some of her enthusiasm dimmed as she drove home, worried about Joshua and his grandfather. Her small apartment usually welcomed her like a warm hug, but it felt oddly cold as she let herself in. Feeling too listless to make herself a real meal, she boiled some instant ramen for dinner. She ate in front of the TV, watching a quirky reality show about an antique shop. But even her favorite comfort food and a fun show did nothing to help her relax.

She took her half-eaten ramen to the kitchen and dumped it out in the sink. After she did the dishes, she made herself a hot cup of tea and sat back down on the couch. Giving up her attempt to take her mind off her worries, Angie reached for her phone yet again. There was still no word from Joshua.

Despite her resolve not to bother him—he had enough to deal with—she texted Joshua.

I'm going to wait for you at your place.

He'd given her a key to his condo just in case, and tonight was the perfect time to use it. She changed into a pair of jeans and a light blouse, and headed to the parking lot. She hit the tail end of rush hour traffic and got to Joshua's a bit later than she'd expected. After checking her phone again, she hurried inside.

She doubted he was home, but her heart still raced at the prospect of seeing him.

The condo was dark. Disappointment flooded her even though she knew it was a long shot that he'd be home. He would probably text her from the hospital with news about the surgery before he came back. She walked around, switching the lights on, so Joshua wouldn't have to walk into a dark house.

She sat in front of the piano and ran her fingers over the keys, hoping to feel the warmth of his fingers on them. Her urgency to see Joshua multiplied. Why was she so desperate to see him? Sure, she was worried about him and his grandfather, but that couldn't be everything.

Then she understood. Joshua was finished with his composition, and Mr. Shin would be going home once he recovered from his surgery. Joshua didn't need her to help him through his creative block, and she didn't need to play for his grandfather anymore. Circumstances had necessitated their frequent meetings and brought them closer together. But those circumstances were now resolved. Would this relationship continue even when he didn't need her anymore?

There was still the premiere left. He would want to watch her introduce his new music to the world. What then? Wouldn't it make sense for Joshua to neatly wrap up their brief affair at the conclusion of everything they'd been working toward? After all, he didn't love her. They weren't meant to last.

A sob lodged itself in her throat, and her heart cracked open. Despite telling herself that she couldn't fall in love with Joshua because he would never love her back, she'd gone and done just that. Maybe she had never stopped loving him. She'd hidden from her emotions, her heartache, because she knew she would never have him again. But meeting him at the Neimans' dinner had awakened her dormant feelings for him.

She could've swallowed her pride and gone back home so her father would help the Chamber Music Society. There had been regret in his voice—he missed her. But she chose to involve Joshua because she couldn't stay away from him. She was searching for a way to be in his life again.

But soon there wouldn't be any reason for her to stay in his life. She stood from the piano and crumpled onto the sofa. What was she going to do? Wait for him to end things, then quietly walk out of his life?

Her phone chimed and she grabbed it off the coffee table. It was a text from Joshua.

The surgery went well and Grandfather is stable. I'll be home soon.

She slumped back down on the sofa. *Oh, thank God.* She was so relieved and happy that his grandfather was going to be all right. But she was terrified of how much hope the words *I'll be home soon* created inside her. She wanted to be home to him, because he already was her home.

She loved him and wanted to be with him. *Even if he doesn't love me back?* Maybe her love could be enough for both of them. But she'd promised him to keep love out of the equation…to not complicate things. Didn't she owe it to him to keep her promise? Whatever her reasons, she'd left him. He had every right to protect his heart from her. She couldn't ruin what they had now by telling him she loved him.

"Angie?" Joshua's deep voice snapped her out of her fog. She'd been so lost in her thoughts that she hadn't heard the door open.

She ran to the entryway and into his arms. He tucked her head under his chin and stood holding her for a long while. Finally, he pulled back and dropped a soft kiss on her lips. "Hey."

She kissed him back. "Hey."

"Thank you for coming," he said softly.

"I wanted to make sure you were okay." She cupped his cheek in the palm of her hand. "Are you okay?"

"I'm so relieved the surgery went well, but it was hell waiting." He pulled her back into his arms. "There were some complications and I was scared out of my mind."

"Now it's over and your grandfather is recovering. Everything is going to be okay."

"I know." Joshua dragged in an unsteady breath and blew it out, ruffling her hair. "I know."

"Have you eaten?" She stepped out of his embrace and tugged him toward the living room by his hand. "Do you want me to make something for you?"

"No." At some point, he was the one tugging her to the bedroom. "I just want to hold you."

Once they reached his bed, she helped him undress with tender care and pulled the comforter over his naked body. Then she went to her side of the bed, undressed and slipped under the covers with him. He immediately gathered her into his arms until the entire length of her body was pressed against his. She drew her hand up and down his back, burrowing her cheek into the crook of his arm. The tension seeped out of his body and his breathing evened out.

"I like coming home to you," he murmured, his words slurred by the pull of sleep.

Hope sprung to life inside Angie, piercing her defensive walls. It took all her willpower to smother the hope before it overtook her whole being. His soft snore of exhaustion saved her from answering. It was for the best.

She'd broken his heart once. She didn't deserve another chance.

The music center's lounge hummed with life and excitement as the maestro's circle event got into full swing. Men and women in glittering formal wear mingled and laughed, sipping expensive champagne. The Chamber Music Society didn't skimp when it came to pampering their highest donors.

Joshua gulped down the rest of his champagne, letting his gaze take in the horde of people. He was once more attending as his grandfather's stand-in. Halabuji was recovering speedily from his surgery and wouldn't need his services much longer. Meanwhile, Joshua obligingly mingled with the other patrons at the gathering while stealing glances at Angie.

He wanted to get her alone for a while, away from prying eyes. Sneaking around might have been fun when they were in college, but he didn't have the patience for it now. Even so, they couldn't be seen as more than casual acquaintances in front of her sisters.

She wanted to keep their relationship a secret from them. That way, she wouldn't have to lie outright to her sisters to protect his identity. Joshua understood and appreciated how carefully she guarded his secret, but he had a feeling there was more to it. And he couldn't deny the sliver of hurt that burrowed into his heart. He didn't intend for their relationship to be a brief affair. Not anymore. How long could she hide their involvement from them? Or did she still believe that what they had was a fleeting interlude?

This longing and possessiveness had grown and solidified into a constant obsession since the night of his grandfather's surgery. Walking into his condo and finding her waiting there for him had almost brought him to his knees with gratitude and happiness. And the way she wrapped herself around his body and lent him her strength filled him with a sense of wholeness he'd never felt before. He'd fallen asleep in her arms believing that everything was going to be all right.

Angie looked stunning in her black strapless gown with her hair swept up into a loose chignon, revealing the graceful line of her neck. The Hana Trio had performed beautifully earlier this evening. She still had the afterglow of a successful performance, and his body flooded with heat every time he looked at her.

The musicians stayed for drinks with the patrons

to answer any questions they might have. Angie had been speaking for a while with a silver-haired man with a smarmy smile, and the worm's eyes had never strayed far from her breasts. Joshua quashed the urge to give this guy a good shove. When he met Angie's gaze across the room, her eyes said *Save me*. That was all the encouragement he needed.

"I'm sorry to interrupt," Joshua said as he approached, not sounding sorry at all.

"Well, now… I…" the older man blubbered, suddenly torn away from his ogling.

Joshua turned to face Angie, half blocking her from the other patron. "I wanted to congratulate you on your performance tonight. You and your sisters sounded sublime."

"Thank you, Mr. Shin. You're too kind," she said with a grateful smile.

"May I walk you to the bar for a drink?" He offered her his arm.

"That sounds lovely." She linked her arm through his and turned to the silver-haired ass. "Thank you for your support of the Chamber Music Society."

"It's my pleasure, Ms. Han," the man tried to say graciously, but his pout ruined the effect.

Once they were out of earshot, Angie leaned toward him and whispered, "Thank you for rescuing me. I was seconds away from dumping my champagne over his head to make him stop staring at my cleavage."

"Happy to assist," Joshua said, grinning down at her. When they reached the bar, he handed her a fresh flute of champagne.

She took a sip, her nose wrinkling adorably. “I’m like a kid. I love how the bubbles tickle my throat.”

“You look all grown-up to me,” he said in a low voice.

A deep pink blush stained her cheeks. “Joshua, behave.”

“I don’t think I will,” he whispered with a wolfish grin. “Meet me up those stairs in five minutes.”

“What are you…?”

He walked away from her before she finished. After a quick glance around the crowd to make sure he wouldn’t be noticed, he climbed the stairs to the next floor. And five minutes later Angie joined him.

“What is even up here?” he asked, looking down an austere corridor.

“More importantly, what are we doing up here?” she said. “The executive offices are up here, as well as a small library.”

“Let’s go to the library.” He grabbed her hand and tugged her down the hall.

“We should get back.” Even so, she ran along with him until she dug her heels in and stopped. When he looked askance at her, she opened one of the doors. “This is it. Were you so desperate for a tour?”

“I am desperate.” The private library was small but stacked floor to ceiling with books. The rich crimson-and-gold carpet and the wooden shelves gave a rich, intimate feel to the room. He locked the door behind them. “But not for a tour.”

“Joshua,” she said sternly.

He pushed her up against a shelf and kissed her

deeply, drawing a moan from her. He bent his head and eased her strapless dress down so he could kiss the sweet mounds of her breasts. She buried her hands in his hair and pressed herself against his lips.

A low chuckle escaped him, and a thrill slithered down his back. He loved how responsive she was to his touch and how her passion burned as hotly as his. He knelt at her feet and rose again, drawing her skirt up to her waist. He wanted her and he couldn't wait a second longer. When he looked in her eyes for acquiescence, she gave a quick nod and grabbed his lapels to pull him in for another searing kiss. He tasted champagne in her mouth as her slick tongue tangled with his.

He pushed aside her panties and slid his hand down to her core, and she jerked against him.

"God, you're so wet," he growled, inserting a finger inside her warmth.

"I want you inside me, Joshua."

With trembling hands, he reached for his wallet and sheathed himself before driving into her to the hilt. Angie began to scream and he clamped his hand over her mouth.

"Shh. We need to be quiet."

Slowly, he began pumping into her, her back against the shelf and her legs wrapped tightly around his waist. Her deep moan was muffled behind his hand. When her tongue flicked out and licked his fingers, he groaned quietly and pushed his index finger into her mouth. She sucked on it, pulling it in and out with the rhythm of their coupling.

He was so damn close. He didn't know how much longer he could last.

"I can't hold on…" He shifted her hips and thrust deeper, harder. "Baby, come for me."

Her internal muscles clenched around him and she bit her lips to quiet her cry. All his control broke and he drove wildly into her before collapsing against her as his own climax claimed him.

They stood still until their panting evened out. She spoke first. "I think I quite enjoy being ravished."

"Do you now?" He grinned with satisfaction as he pulled away from her.

"I do." She primly smoothed out her skirt and adjusted her bodice. "How do I look?"

She was flushed and her chignon had come loose, but it wasn't readily apparent that she'd been ravished. "You look beautiful and professional."

She reached out and smoothed his hair. "And you look handsome and rich."

"Good." He chuckled. "Let's go downstairs and resume our roles."

"I'll go downstairs first. You could come down a few minutes later, okay?"

"Sounds like a plan." He spun her around and patted her bottom to urge her along.

With one last smile over her shoulder, she slipped out of the library. With his heart pounding inside him, he knew he would remember that smile for the rest of his life.

Eleven

Angie focused on the road and attempted to shake off the sense of impending doom that everything was coming to a close. It was a good thing that Mr. Shin would be discharged tomorrow. She was so happy that he was well enough to go home. But tonight would be the last time she performed for him at the hospital. Then her brief stint as a music therapist would come to an end.

She parked her car a good distance away from the main entrance of the hospital. It was silly. But it would be the last time Joshua walked her to her car like this...she wanted it to last as long as possible. She gave her head a firm shake. She was acting as though this would be the last time she saw him. Just the thought alone was enough to make her heart tear and bleed.

Her trek to the entrance was a slow crawl and her cello felt double its weight. She needed to stop feeling sorry for herself. She wanted to give Mr. Shin a performance he wouldn't forget. With her chin held high, she walked into the lobby and froze to the spot.

Joshua was waiting for her, typing furiously into his phone. She guessed it was an urgent business matter because two deep grooves had formed between his eyebrows, which always happened when he was intensely focused on something. She didn't want to disturb him, so she stood where she was until he lifted his head.

The smile that spread across his face made her heart soar. She ran the rest of the way to him and flung herself into his arms. With an "oof," he caught her in a tight embrace and lifted her off her feet, chuckling low in his chest.

"I missed you," she whispered.

His laughter quieted and his arms tightened around her. "I missed you, too."

Both joy and a boundless sadness filled her. She was his for now. That was all that mattered, but her heart screamed that it wasn't enough.

What is it that you want?

She wanted everything. But he'd once entrusted her with his heart, and she shattered it to pieces. What right did she have to ask him to trust her again? To love her again?

And if she ever got his assurance that this was more than a short-lived affair, she would have to tell her sisters the truth about her relationship with Joshua. Telling them that he was A.S. wasn't the problem—she trusted her sisters to keep his secret safe—but how could she tell them about their past? She would have to break their hearts by revealing a side to their father they would be better off not knowing. Their father might lose the closeness he shared with her sisters when they were all he had. She didn't wish that on him even if she couldn't forgive him for taking Joshua away from her. Maybe it was really better this way—this way no one got hurt. Except for her.

She pulled back from his embrace and linked her free hand with his. "So how's your grandfather doing?"

"He says he's feeling like a million bucks." Joshua grinned at her, smoothing his thumb back and forth over the back of her hand. "He's excited to be going home tomorrow."

When they arrived at the older man's hospital room, he welcomed Angie with open arms. She hugged him tight, emotion clogging her throat. She hadn't seen him since the surgery and she was grateful he was doing so well.

"You look well, Halabuji," she said, grasping his hand.

"What did I tell you? I told you I'll get better." He laughed and patted her hand. "I'm a man of my word."

"Is it selfish of me to be a little sad that I won't be able to play for you anymore?"

"I'm going to miss you, too, my dear." He glanced between her and Joshua. "But I have a feeling I'll be seeing you often."

Her cheeks burning, she sneaked a peek at Joshua, who smiled affectionately at his grandfather. "Stop teasing her, Halabuji. She's not here to be pestered by you."

"Insolent boy," his grandfather said mock sternly. "But you *are* here to play for me and there's nothing else I'd like better."

"There are a few pieces left on your list..." She sat down and positioned her cello.

"It's too hard to decide. You play everything so beautifully. I honestly could listen to you play scales all day."

"You sweet-talker." She laughed. "Why don't we make it a medley?"

"That sounds like the perfect solution," the patient heartily agreed.

Joshua watched the exchange with an amused smile. When their eyes met, he gave her a playful wink. "Classical music lovers sure know how to rock it."

With her heart close to bursting, she played some songs sure to please, like "My Favorite Things" and "Over the Rainbow," but she ended the medley with a beloved classical piece, "The Swan," by Saint-Saëns.

Joshua and his grandfather clapped resoundingly, and the hospital staff gathered outside the door joined in. Angie blinked in surprise when one of the nurses entered and handed her a small bouquet.

"For me? I don't know what to say." She buried her nose in the flowers and breathed deeply.

"Ed was an absolute delight to have in our ward, but you coming to play for him was an extraspecial bonus for us," the nurse said earnestly.

"Thank you so much," Angie said, turning toward the door to include the other staff.

The nurse who gave her the flowers was the last to leave the room after checking on the patient.

"It looks like you provided music therapy for more than just me," Mr. Shin said in a pleased voice.

"I'm happy so many people got to enjoy my music."

"And more people will be able to listen to you play once the season begins." Joshua's grandfather scratched his chin. "Everyone seems to be aflutter over the premiere of that fellow A.S.'s new string trio."

She almost sprained her eyeballs to keep her gaze from flitting to Joshua. "Yes, the Chamber Music Society is very excited as well."

"I'm not so sure about him. He's a little bit too modern for me," A.S.'s grandfather declared.

Angie pressed her lips together to hold back her laugh, but one look at Joshua staring valiantly at the ceiling almost made her lose it. She cleared her throat. "Give him a try. He grows on you."

After they said their good-nights, Angie and Joshua walked out to the parking lot. The night air was cool against her skin, but her briefly forgotten doomsday mood overtook her again. This was their last walk to her car… Her steps were heavy but Joshua matched her pace and walked slowly beside her, not seeming to mind.

"He grows on you?" He bumped her with his shoulder.

Despite herself, she laughed. "What? I just wanted him to give you a chance."

"My own grandfather." Joshua shook his head with a wry smile.

"Do you plan on telling him someday?" she asked.

"Maybe, but not now." His expression turned somber. "I don't want to worry him."

"Worry him?"

He hesitated for a moment before he answered, "The board of directors is appointing Riddle's new CEO soon but… I have competition."

"I overheard your grandfather mention something about that…" she said. "But what does that have to do with you being A.S.?"

"If I told my grandfather right now, he might worry that my competition will find out about my identity and use it against me to win the CEO seat."

"Use it against you?" Alarm snaked through her. "How?"

"He'll try to convince the board of directors that I'm not committed to Riddle."

"But that's not true. There is no reason why you can't compose *and* run your company."

"I'm not sure what the board will believe with Nathan Whitley twisting the facts." Joshua sighed. "That's why I can't afford to have anyone find out who I am."

"Why didn't you tell me any of this before?"

"The same reason I haven't told my grandfather that I'm A.S." He offered her a crooked smile. "I didn't want you to worry."

"Oh, Joshua." It hurt her to think he'd been carrying this burden all on his own.

When they reached her car, he kissed her deeply until they were both breathless. "Come home with me."

"After that kiss, I'm not going anywhere else." She stared wide-eyed at him.

"Then I'll be sure to kiss you like that every night." His smile was all male pride and arrogance.

Every night? She steeled herself against the burst of hope. He didn't mean anything by it.

They drove in separate cars to his condo. As usual, Joshua got there first and was waiting for her in the lobby. When they got into the elevator, he pressed her up against the wall and kissed her until she was burning up inside. Luckily, no one interrupted them.

As soon as the door to his place closed behind them, Joshua lifted her into his arms and headed to the bedroom. They tore at each other's clothes and tumbled onto the bed in a mad rush. She pushed him onto his back and straddled him. He held himself still and waited for her to make the next move, but his fingers dug into her hips.

"God, Angie," he growled. "I want you so much."

"And I want you," she said huskily.

Heady with power, she slowly lowered herself onto him, rocking and swerving her hips, until a tortured groan left his lips. For a while, he let her set the pace, but soon he gripped her hips and surged into her faster and harder. As they reached their climax together, they shouted each other's names, then collapsed onto the bed, wrecked and winded.

Once she caught her breath, she said, "Are you sure you want to kiss me like that *every* night?"

"Every fucking night," he said in a satisfied drawl and kissed her bare shoulder. "I can't get enough of you."

Joshua wanted her. But how long would that last? When the first flush of desire faded, what would they have left? No matter how hard she tried to deny it, a relationship built on a flitting attraction wasn't enough for her. Not anymore. She loved him and wanted forever with him.

She wouldn't let fear hold her back. If she had shared everything with him ten years ago, they might never have parted. She had to tell him how she felt about him—tell him that she loved him. Maybe he would be able to trust her with his heart again.

But what about her sisters and their father? Her sisters were strong and she trusted them to make the right decisions. All those years ago, she chose her mom over Joshua—over herself—and sacrificed their love. This time she was going to choose him no matter what. She was going to put their love above all else.

She deserved another chance. *They* deserved another chance.

Joshua stepped out of his condo the next morning, feeling a little off. Nights spent without Angie had that effect on him. She had gone back to her apartment last night because of an early morning rehearsal.

After pushing the button for the elevator, he pulled out his phone to take it off silent mode. He blinked at the screen. It seemed as though every notification possible was crowding his screen—emails, messages and phone calls.

Five of the phone calls were from his assistant, Janice. And there was also a text message from her.

Please give me a call before you come into the office.

The elevator doors opened but he stood where he was and dialed his assistant's number.

"Joshua." She answered on the first ring.

"What's going on, Janice?" He looked impatiently at his watch, wondering if he would be late for his morning meeting.

"It's…the news…" She had nerves of steel and was never at a loss for words. An ominous sense of wrongness settled over him. "They know who you are. Well, we all do now."

"You're not making any sense." His blood pounded in his ears and his fingers tightened around the phone. "Start from the beginning."

"The news is everywhere." She took an unsteady breath. "They're saying that you're the anonymous composer A.S."

Joshua's stomach dropped to the floor and he widened his stance to steady himself. After several attempts, he got his voice to work. "What's the situation at work?"

"It's not quite nine yet, but several board members have called and a couple executives have already come by. Once the workday starts, I have a feeling the phone is going to be ringing off the hook and there'll be a line outside your door."

"Janice, thank you for letting me know…and for not asking any questions. I'll tell you everything once I get into the office."

With his mind in a cloud of panic, he went back inside his condo on autopilot. Then he stood in the middle of the living room not knowing what to do… not knowing what to think. He hadn't meant to keep his identity a secret indefinitely, but he'd wanted to reveal it on his own time—on his own terms—after the CEO appointment.

But his worst fears had come to pass. He might lose his chance to become Riddle's next CEO. His family's legacy might be lost because of his choices. What must his parents think? And Halabuji…he didn't need this shock so soon after his surgery.

How had this happened? No one knew his identity. He'd made sure of that. No one other than… Angie. His heartbeat picked up and he began pacing. He shouldn't jump to nonsensical conclusions.

But she'd betrayed him once. Why wouldn't she do it again? No, that had been for her sick mother. She had no reason to betray him. How could he even suspect her? He shook his head to clear it. She'd helped him through his creative block to compose the new string trio. She'd helped his grandfather's recovery with such generosity and kindness. And what about their relationship? They might not be in love, but what they had was real. Wasn't it?

"Joshua?" Angie's voice rang out from the hallway. It didn't occur to him to answer. He just stood where he was as she ran into the living room looking left and right. "Joshua."

She wrapped her arms around his waist and pressed herself against him, burying her face in his chest. He pulled her close and soaked up the solace she offered despite his splintered thoughts. He needed to calm down and think logically, but he was spinning out of control without anything to anchor him.

"I saw the news." She leaned back and stared up at him with concern and soft sympathy in her eyes. "Are you okay?"

"I… I don't know…" His mind spun in a blur of confused thoughts.

"We'll figure something out. It's going to be okay." She searched his face. "Do you know how this happened?"

"I have no idea." His gaze flitted away from her. "You're the only person who knows."

With a warm hand on his cheek, she turned him to face her again. "You know I would never reveal your secret, right?"

"Ri…right." He hesitated for the briefest second but the blood drained out of her face. "Of course. Of course, I know you wouldn't."

She stepped out of his arms and retreated to the

opposite side of the living room. "But you considered the possibility."

It wasn't a question. He couldn't even deny it. "I..."

"Did you believe it?" Hurt and anger snapped in her eyes. "Even for a second?"

"I don't...know," he said haltingly. Had he believed, however briefly, that she had betrayed him again? "Like I said, you're the only person who knows I'm A.S."

"You didn't answer my question. Did you believe that I leaked your secret?"

"I said I don't know." He threw his hands up in the air, suddenly defensive and scared. "Maybe you needed to drum up more media attention for the Chamber Music Society... The upcoming season is so important..."

Her sharp gasp stopped his blabber. "You thought I betrayed you for the society?"

"It's not important. It was just a passing thought." He ran his hand down his face. Where was she going with this? "I told you I know you weren't the one who revealed my identity."

"No, it *is* important because it shows you still don't trust me," she said, her voice breaking. "It's important because I love you, and...and I need you to trust me."

"You love me?" His heart hammered as joy threatened to take flight in his soul but he immediately crushed it.

"Yes," she whispered through pale lips. "I never stopped loving you."

"But we agreed to keep love out of our relationship." His accusation lingered in the air between them.

"I lied to myself so I could hold on to you as long as possible." Silent tears rolled down her cheeks.

"I told you I couldn't make any promises." Love was dangerous. Love could break him.

"I know." She wiped her tears away with both her hands. "I did this to myself."

She was hurting and he was the one hurting her, but he couldn't stop. He couldn't tell her what she wanted to hear. "You shouldn't have fallen in love with me."

"And I'm sorry I can't be here for you." Fresh tears filled her eyes and spilled down her face. "But now I know I wouldn't have been much help to you. You need someone you love—someone you trust—by your side. And I'm neither of those things."

"What are you saying?" His body shook with fear that began at his core.

"I'm saying I love you—" she took a shuddering breath "—but I can't be with you."

"You can't or you won't?" He clamped his mouth shut when she flinched. "What we have is good enough. We don't need love to complicate things."

"It's not good enough for me," she said with quiet strength. "Goodbye, Joshua."

"Please." He reached out for her but she was already turning her back to him.

When he heard the quiet click of the door shutting behind her, he stumbled onto the sofa because his legs couldn't hold him up. It wasn't supposed to hurt like this. Why did he hurt like this when he didn't love her? The answer was glaringly clear but he refused to face it. He laughed, a barren and hopeless sound. It was over. She was gone.

Numbness overtook him, and he welcomed it.

Twelve

Angie had to concentrate on the road. She couldn't let her emotions breach the dam she had erected until she was in a safe place. *Gas, blinker, brake, stop. Check the mirrors, change lanes, gas, brake.* She parked a bit too far from the curb, but it was the best she could do.

She got out of her car and walked to the intercom on unstable legs. *Please be home. Please be home.*

"Who is it?" Chloe asked through the intercom.

"It's me," she said shakily. Hearing her sister's voice almost undid her, but she had to keep it together until she was off the street. She had to hang on tight just a bit longer.

"Angie? Come on up."

She put one foot in front of the other until she got

to Chloe's door. She knocked erratically. When the door opened and her sister's lovely face appeared in front of her, Angie fell into her arms, and the tears she'd held back poured out of her in a torrent of grief.

"Shh. You're okay." Her sister patted her back and held her tight. "You're okay."

When Angie's knees buckled, Chloe grabbed her by the waist and swung her limp arm over her shoulder to support her. Together they swayed and tripped as they made their way to the sofa. Luckily for them, Chloe's cozy graduate housing didn't require them to travel far.

Her baby sister laid her down on the couch, putting a pillow under her head and pulling a blanket over her. "I'm going to call Megan, then make you a nice cup of tea."

Angie tried to nod but all she could do was blink. With another worried glance, Chloe hurried to the kitchen, tapping on her phone. Her kitchen was only ten steps from the couch, but her muffled voice sounded far away. "Megan, it's me. I think you should come over."

Her sister's voice faded away and was replaced by Joshua's hard words. *You shouldn't have fallen in love with me.* Angie placed her hands over her ears and shut her eyes, but she still heard his voice and saw the accusation chiseled into his face.

The hope she'd been cradling in her heart dimmed and flickered out. She was cold. It was a brittle, biting cold that tore jaggedly into her bones. And she was so very tired. The fatigue slowly, slowly weighed her down, and she let the oblivion of sleep erase the nightmare in her mind.

"She wasn't even like this when we lost Mom," Chloe whispered.

"She was trying to be strong for us," Megan said. "I heard her sob night after night when she thought we were all asleep."

"But how could someone so strong crumble like this? What could've happened?" Her youngest sister's voice trembled slightly.

"Don't worry, Chloe. She'll tell us what happened when she's ready, and we'll be here for her. Whatever it is, we'll help her get through it."

Megan's calm reassurance dulled the pain that threatened to engulf her once she let her consciousness return fully. She couldn't sleep forever. She needed to come back to her sisters even if she bled from the pain.

"I think she's awake." Chloe was jumped to her feet and was by her side in an instant.

With her baby sister's help, Angie pushed herself up into a sitting position. Then Megan and Chloe sat down on either side of her, each grabbing one of her hands.

"I don't know what happened, but we're here for you, Unni," Megan promised.

"And if you need us to beat anyone up, I'll happily kick some ass," Chloe said, trying to draw a smile out of Angie, but she didn't know if she would ever smile again.

"I love him." Her words left her dry mouth in a hoarse rasp. Chloe handed her the cup of water she had ready at the coffee table. Her sisters sat quietly and waited for her to continue. "I'm in love with Joshua Shin."

They looked at each other with wide eyes, then back at her.

"But the state you're in…does it have something to do with him being A.S.?" Megan gently prodded when Angie stopped to stare off into space.

"A part of him believes that I leaked the secret," Angie murmured. A strange kind of numbness was seeping into her. "He doesn't trust me."

"You already knew he was A.S.?" Chloe squeezed her hand. "Unni, you need to tell us from the beginning so we can understand."

The beginning. The first time she saw Joshua, he was laughing in the hallway of the music building. His head was thrown back and the strong column of his throat worked as laughter flowed out of him. He was so beautiful, he took her breath away. He was the first boy who had made her feel that way. If his eyes hadn't met hers across the hallway that day, would she not be hurting so much today?

She needed her sisters. Their love and support had helped her overcome her grief over their mother's death. She needed them to survive this. They had to know everything, so she started from the beginning.

Other than to squeeze her hand and wipe away her tears, her sisters let her talk without interruption. She broke down a few times while telling her story, but at last she got it all out. Then she cried. She let go of the last of her control and sobbed brokenly, mourning the loss of love and hope. And she hurt for Joshua. She hurt for what they could've been…so very much.

Her sisters hugged her from each side, and they sat quietly like that until her tears ebbed and her shaking eased. Angie felt hollowed out, but the burning pain in her heart had numbed with exhaustion.

"I had no idea Appa did that to you. I'm so sorry, Unni." Chloe's voice broke on the last words.

Out of the three of them, she was the closest to their father and he cherished her, his baby girl. Hearing how he'd treated Angie had to be shocking and painful for her.

"Chloe, you shouldn't let what happened between Appa and me to influence your relationship with him." Angie took a deep breath and continued, "He was distraught with Mom's diagnosis, and he didn't trust Joshua. Maybe he thought Joshua was only using me to get information about our company… I don't know. But I believe in his own way, Appa was trying to protect me. I think I'm beginning to forgive him."

Megan scoffed angrily but didn't say anything.

"Don't worry about me," Chloe quickly added. "Are *you* going to be okay?"

"I don't know." Tears filled her eyes again. Megan rubbed her back and made soothing noises as Angie cried quietly into her hand.

She didn't put on a brave face to protect her sisters. There was a crack in her soul that was growing bit by bit, and soon she would split in two. Her sisters had to help hold her together.

"I should've told him how I felt about him before this happened. I wanted to… I was going to…but I kept making excuses about the timing." Angie tore little pieces off the ball of tissue she was holding. "If I'd been braver, I would've told him and our relationship might've had a real chance."

"Or you could've lost what you had together," Megan said, tucking a strand of Angie's hair behind her ear. "He was adamant that he didn't want love and commitment from your relationship. Who in their right mind would find confessing their love easy in that situation?"

"The right thing to do is sometimes the hardest thing to do," Angie murmured.

"Even at a time like this, she's dropping nuggets of wisdom. Our older sister, ladies and gentlemen," Chloe quipped, linking her arm through Angie's.

Angie's watery laugh turned into a hiccup. "And I did the right thing today."

"But you love him…" Chloe said, the rims of her eyes turning red.

"I do." *With all my heart.* Angie swallowed the sob welling in her throat. She had to be strong. "But holding on to hope will destroy me. He'll never love me. I have to accept that and move on. That's the only way I can survive this."

Joshua left his condo with enough time to have an hour to spare before the board of directors' meeting. He had spent the last few days pouring over the arguments he intended to present to them. Nathan Whitley was reacting exactly as anticipated, bringing into question Joshua's ability to lead Riddle Incorporated when he had such an involved "hobby" on the side. The board members who already doubted his competence because of his age might be swayed by Whitley's baseless claims. To distract himself from his frustration, he turned on the radio to a local news station.

He listened with half an ear to the weather and traffic update. Then the public radio station thanked its supporters and sponsors before moving on to the latest news.

"Joshua Shin, the heir apparent to Riddle Incorporated, a thriving electronic components company in Los Angeles, has been revealed to be the famed composer, A.S. Despite the success of his work, Shin kept his identity as the composer a secret. The question is why? What had—"

He impatiently switched to his favorite classical station. He'd forgotten that he *was* the latest news for the time being. When the music ended, the host of the morning show introduced the upcoming piece.

"Next is a work by A.S., or shall we say, Joshua Shin—"

He turned off the radio altogether and sat through the traffic, drumming an agitated beat on the steering wheel with his fingers. He had to tune out all that noise. The media could speculate all they want. All that mattered was convincing the board of directors that appointing him as Riddle's next CEO was the best thing they could do for the company.

He had to focus on that and only that. He'd shut the door on everything else. Joshua fought to hold back his dammed-up emotions. He would collapse from their weight if he gave in.

Janice was waiting for him with a stack of files when he got to his office.

"Is everything ready?" he asked, heading straight for his desk.

"Yes, I made copies of the key graphs and charts for your presentation. The board members will have it right in front of them when you drive the point home."

"Thank you, Janice."

When she shut the door behind her, Joshua focused his attention on preparing for the board of directors meeting. He was still the best man for the CEO position. Being A.S. didn't change that fact. The board members needed reassurance of his competence and commitment to the company. Especially the ones who were already on the fence about his appointment. He intended to give them that reassurance.

A quick glance at his watch told him that it was game time. He fixed his tie, put on his jacket and walked out of his office, ready to get the job done. Once the meeting was called into session, Joshua went to stand at the head of the table and met the eyes of each of the board members. His father and grandfather weren't among them. They hadn't come. A muscle jumped in his jaw.

He'd visited his parents and grandfather the evening after the news broke. Despite their shock, his grandfather and mother were willing to listen, but his father just stared at the wall in front of him—not even acknowledging his presence.

Joshua had explained that music was a part of him and suppressing it would suffocate his soul—it was who he was. But he also reassured them that over the past few years, Riddle and its employees had come to mean the world to him. He wanted to continue his grandfather's and father's legacy. And he had no doubt that he had it in him to succeed at both music and business. They just needed to trust him.

Their absence was their answer. They didn't trust him. It felt like a physical blow and he gripped the edge of the table for support. But he had to pull himself together. He still had a job to do.

Just then, his father and grandfather entered the conference room. Other than the cane he was leaning on, Halabuji looked every bit his formidable self. And his father, the current CEO, walked in like he owned the room. They took their seats in the sudden hush.

Then his father met Joshua's eyes from across the table and gave him a firm nod. A pressing weight lifted from his chest and Joshua faced the board members with renewed determination.

"Let's skip the preamble and get to the crux of this meeting. I've been Riddle Incorporated's vice president of operations for the last three years, and the company's corresponding growth is irrefutable." Joshua's voice rang with confidence. "I've gathered some data for your review."

He clicked through the slides, pointing out key projects and contracts that contributed to the company's growth.

"I realize the news that I'm A.S. comes as a shock to many of you, but if you take a step back and reflect on it, you'll see that my competence as Riddle's future CEO shouldn't come into question." He paused for a moment. "The fact of the matter is I've been composing as A.S. the entire time I've been Riddle's Vice President of Operations." Murmurs rippled through the room. "Being a composer has not and will not hinder my ability to lead this company. You all have just seen concrete evidence of this fact."

"The CEO position isn't only about competence. It's about commitment," Richard Benson spoke up. "It's obvious music is your passion. Riddle Incorporated is just an afterthought for you."

"Riddle has been in my family for three generations. My love of music doesn't diminish the fact that I would do anything to protect my family's legacy," Joshua said with utmost sincerity.

"And is it Nathan Whitley's *passion* that has him moving from corporation to corporation every three, four years?" his father asked. "Or is the fattest compensation package driving his migration?"

"This meeting isn't about Mr. Whitley." Scott Grey loudly cleared his throat and addressed Joshua. "Have you ever thought about the impact your *other job* could have on Riddle?"

"The positive or the negative?" his grandfather interjected. "This presentation provided cold hard facts that being a composer hasn't negatively impacted his effectiveness as an executive of Riddle. As for the positive, I believe the media is quite captivated with the idea of Riddle's future CEO being a true Renaissance man."

"I'll be sure to explore that marketing angle in the future, Grandfather," Joshua said, making a show of jotting down the idea in his notebook. "If there are no more questions, I'll conclude my presentation. Thank you for your time."

"Thank you, Mr. Shin. I'm sure everyone here agrees that our questions have been satisfactorily answered. We'll vote for Riddle Incorporated's new CEO," Clarice Wong looked over at Joshua and held his gaze for an unblinking moment, "at the next regularly scheduled board meeting. This meeting is adjourned."

Joshua had done everything he could to make sure he was still in the running for the CEO position. He hoped it was enough. Several board members shook his hand before going on their way. As the conference room emptied out, he walked up to his father and grandfather.

"Thank you for trusting me." His voice was thick with emotion. "I won't let you down."

"I know you won't," his father said simply.

"And Angie was right about your music." His grandfather coughed, his eyes red with unshed tears. "A.S.'s music does grow on you."

Joshua looked at the two men he looked up to most in this world and smiled. He could face anything with them by his side.

"Now, get back to work." His father stood from his

chair. “I’m still the CEO of this company. Don’t let me see you slacking off.”

Joshua returned to his office and fell into his chair. Along with the relief from his successful presentation, exhaustion rolled in, threatening to flatten him. He’d hardly slept since the news broke, and most of his energy had been spent on protecting his family’s legacy and keeping his emotions at bay.

He lasted until the end of the day by losing himself in work. His feet felt like they were encased in cement as he made his way to his car, and cold sweat broke out on his forehead as he drove home.

A few steps away from his condo, he stumbled and caught himself against the hallway wall. He walked the rest of the way with his hand on the wall, then leaned against the door as he unlocked it with unsteady hands. He took a step inside his condo, then another before he fell to his knees.

He had no strength left in him to stem the tide of emotions that crashed into him. Regret. Grief. Loss. More than anything, loss tore away at him. *Angie.* She was gone.

Joshua pushed himself off the floor and grabbed a bottle of Scotch from the bar. He slumped down on the sofa and took a long swig straight from the bottle. Heat burned down his throat and settled in his stomach. He took another swig. He couldn’t get drunk fast enough.

It hurt. It was too much to bear. He’d lost her once and it had broken him. This time, he’d sworn he would guard his heart so she wouldn’t be able to hurt him. But he was the one who had hurt her, driving a knife into his own heart in the process. He'd lost her again. He tilted back the bottle and drank, hoping the Scotch would help dull the pain. It didn't.

Had he truly believed for even a second that she'd betrayed him? He huffed a humorless laugh. Not even for a second. Then why couldn't he have just told her that? Because he was a coward. For a decade, he'd believed that she left him because she cared more about money than him. And when they met again, he feared that she would walk away from him any time it served her better. Even after learning the truth—that it broke her heart to leave him—he was so afraid of getting hurt again that he'd pushed her away. He'd let her believe that he didn't trust her.

Oh, God. She loved him. She'd offered him her heart and he'd thrown the beautiful gift back in her face. It gutted him to imagine how much he'd hurt her but he couldn't let himself drown in the pain. He had to fix this. He had to make things right and win her back because...he was in love with her.

Joshua had been too afraid to face his feelings because he didn't think he could survive another heartbreak. But what he really couldn't survive was living a lifetime without her.

Even if it was too late—*God, don't let it be too late*—he wanted her to know that he loved her more than anything in the world. That he trusted her with his heart and soul. He was willing to risk everything if it meant having her. Fear would not hold him back anymore.

Thirteen

"Knock, knock," Angie announced herself as she walked through the open door of Janet's office.

Her mentor pulled off her reading glasses and stood up to hug her. "Hello, my dear. How are you?"

"I'm fine," she said automatically, even though it wasn't true. It had been close to a month since she left Joshua but her wound still felt raw. "How about you?"

"Working my tail off for the season opening. It's exhausting but exhilarating at the same time."

"I have to confess I'm a little nervous." Angie settled herself in one of the guest chairs. "You usually don't call me into your office unless you want to talk business."

"Well, this could be good news or bad news, depending on how you look at it," Janet said enigmatically.

"That's not helping. Please just tell me."

"A.S. came in to see Thomas yesterday afternoon with a proposal," her mentor said. Angie's heart dipped as though she was speeding down a roller coaster. "He wants the music he wrote for the Hana Trio to be returned to him."

"What? No." Devastation crashed into Angie.

Did Joshua resent her so much that he would risk the Chamber Music Society's survival to punish her? Didn't he understand it would've hurt her too much to stay with him knowing that he didn't trust her? That he didn't love her?

"He wants it returned because he had a sudden inspiration for a new piece that was perfect for the trio." Janet gazed steadily at her. "He hopes you agree once you see the music."

Angie was speechless. The roller coaster was making a slow climb and she didn't know how far the fall might be. Why would he write another piece? What did he want?

"I know that only leaves you with a couple of weeks to practice it, but you girls can do it," her mentor soothed, thinking her silence was a sign of her concern.

"Of course," Angie said with more confidence than she felt. "We'll make time for extra practices and get the piece ready for opening night."

"I never did ask you how you knew A.S.," Janet began gently, "but I can't help but think that there's some history between the two of you. In addition to writing a new piece for the Hana Trio, he offered to conduct one of his own pieces with the chamber orchestra on opening night. I think his eagerness to help the society has to do with his dedication to you."

"I… I can't…" Angie stuttered. Why was he doing this? She was barely starting to function again. She couldn't do this. She couldn't hope. "I'll tell you someday, but I can't right now."

"As I told you before, you don't need to tell me anything you're not ready to. Just know that I'm always here for you." Janet handed her a folder of sheet music. "Here's the new piece. Let me know if you need anything."

Clutching the folder to her chest, Angie bid a hasty farewell and headed for the parking lot. Once she was sitting in her car, she opened the folder and pulled out the music. Despite her turmoil, she couldn't wait to see what he'd done. Maybe he'd written a new piece because *they* had worked on the other one together. Sadness threatened to overwhelm her, but she pushed it aside. No more feeling sorry for herself.

Her eyes flitted through the notes, and she felt her excitement grow. It was brilliant. Truly brilliant. Joshua's talent was a gift to the world. Despite everything, she was so proud of him.

She headed straight home. Her fingertips were tingling with the urge to play the new piece, and her foot grew heavy on the gas pedal. For the first time in weeks, a flutter of excitement touched her heart, and the world lost some of its dull, gray cast.

Angie loved coming home, but today it felt as though she had reached an oasis after wandering in the desert for days. When she let herself in, she quickly slipped her shoes off and ran to open the curtains to let in the afternoon light. Then she went to her practice corner and placed the new string trio on her music stand. She removed her cello from its case, and took a deep breath to quiet her mind. From the moment her bow touched the strings, she was sucked into another world. It was a world where only music existed and she was part of the music.

Through the flowing melody, she saw the first sparks of attraction between her and Joshua as they fought to deny it. Then the fire caught, making it impossible to ignore the attraction. The fire spread and grew into a bonfire just as their passion had caught and burned between them. They couldn't get enough of each other. It was a thirst that couldn't be quenched. The notes grew strong and powerful and her body moved with the music.

Then the fire settled into a smooth, flowing form—still hot and fiery—but calmer. That was when their relationship grew into something more, and her feelings for Joshua grew. Every moment they shared was warm and precious, and her heart blossomed with the glow of happiness. The music became rich, more melodic. It was beautiful.

She had anticipated what would come next. The storm. The sky tore open and rain pounded on the fire. The smooth flames twisted in agony, steam floating off the dying embers. The deep, dark strains of the music became frantic, tragic. She didn't know when she started crying but tears streamed down her cheeks.

Her heart clenched and she couldn't take a full breath. The rhythm grew faster and faster, then screeched to an abrupt halt.

There were three bars of rest but the quiet was filled with the beating of her heart. Then poignant, tender notes filled the silence, and she heard the sound of hope. Against all odds, the next soft, gentle wave of music coaxed the fire back to life. And the piece ended with a last hopeful note hanging in the air, like a tendril of smoke rising into the sky.

Angie put aside her cello and buried her face in her hands. Sobs wracked her body. The new string trio touched her to the core of her soul. She saw her love for Joshua in it, and improbably, his love for her. Why would he do this to her? What did he want from her?

Maybe it had nothing to do with her. This brilliant music might've been born out of his newfound freedom. With his identity revealed, his creativity had been unleashed. This piece might be telling a completely different story from what she heard. It had to be. She would be a fool if she believed it could be anything else. She was meant to play the music and she would do that. And that would be all.

She purposefully walked over to the side table for some tissues and blew her nose. Enough crying. Even though it was the music that had made her cry, it was also because it reminded her of Joshua and their relationship. Well, no more crying over him. She had to move on.

Then she cried again in the shower. She felt a bit rebellious about it by then. It had only been a month.

Didn't she have the right to take some time to get over losing the love of her life for the second time?

Without bothering to dry it, she piled her hair on top of her head in a messy bun and put on some well-worn sweats that hung off her body. She hadn't been able to eat lately. She sighed and headed to the kitchen to reheat some chicken soup Megan had made for her when she was here a couple nights ago.

Her sisters have been taking turns checking in on her. A part of her wanted to be left alone, but she wasn't doing a very good job taking care of herself, so she was grateful for her sisters' fussing.

Angie took the bowl of soup to the dining room table and sat down to eat. She swirled her spoon around and around to let it cool a bit.

She missed Joshua so much. She desperately wanted to see his handsome face. But would she still want to see his face if it was shadowed with accusation and resentment? She didn't know.

She wished she'd been braver and confessed her love to him sooner. But he had seemed shocked and appalled when she told him. They'd agreed to keep love out of the equation, but their relationship had been real. They had cared about each other and understood each other. Didn't that count for something? And even without the words, she had loved him. Had he not felt it? Had he not returned the feeling in some way?

No. Even if she'd told him she loved him before the secret was out, he wouldn't have been able to love her back. How could there be love without trust? There was never any hope for them. Maybe it was for the best that he'd broken her heart now.

The soup had turned cold before she even tasted it. Suddenly, she couldn't force herself to swallow a single spoonful. She pushed back her chair and went to lie down on the living room couch, her slippered feet scuffing the floor. She couldn't stand being alone with her thoughts, so she turned on her favorite classical music station. The music soothed her like nothing else could and her eye lids grew heavy. Sleep would be a welcome escape. She began drifting off…

"We have a special guest for you today. We know who the anonymous composer A.S. is. But now we get to meet the man who discovered A.S.'s true identity."

Angie sat up so quickly that a pang of dizziness swept through her. The man, a journalist for a small magazine, explained how he'd been searching for A.S.'s identity for the past couple years. She stopped listening when he went on about stumbling upon a shell corporation and a business account. And there it was. Proof that she wasn't the one who had leaked his identity.

If he still had doubts about her involvement in leaking his secret, Joshua would soon learn that she wasn't the one who sold him out. Then what? Would he regret doubting her? Would he regret casting aside her love as though it was an inconvenience to him? It didn't matter. None of it mattered.

It was too late.

* * *

Joshua dug the heels of his palms into his blurry eyes then refocused on the computer screen in front of him. It was close to the end of the day and weariness bore down on him. He'd come into the office at seven in the morning even though he'd been there until 2:00 a.m. the night before. Cleaning up the issues following his unveiling as A.S. had taken time away from his duties at Riddle, and a mountain of work awaited him.

He'd done an interview with a trusted local news station to tell the story of his journey as a composer and corporate executive from his own perspective. There was no point in hiding from the media at this point. It was better to face them on his own terms to stem any rumors or speculations. Any remaining questions should be resolved once the interview aired.

The screen blurred in front of him and he rubbed his tired eyes. The grueling hours weren't strictly necessary, but work distracted him from thinking about Angie. He missed her so much. It was as though he was deprived of something essential to his life, to his survival.

He gave in to the urge to check his phone again. No missed calls. It was foolish to wait for her call, but he couldn't help himself. What did he expect? That Angie was going to see the new string trio he wrote and immediately understand that he loved her? And call to tell him she loved him, too? He huffed a humorless laugh.

There had been no creative block this time. The

music had come to him as naturally as a breeze blowing through the trees. He'd been immature to think that music and Angie existed as one synergetic force—that losing her meant that he would lose his music, too. He understood now that his love of music was his alone. Nothing could take it away from him except for his own stubbornness. Perhaps he had been grasping at whatever excuse he could find to stop himself from falling in love with Angie. But that had been a hopeless cause from the start.

It was his denial of his feelings for Angie that had paralyzed him from composing the first string trio. He had bound and gagged his soul so he wouldn't have to admit that he loved her. How could he have composed like that? Music was born from his soul after all. Once his soul was freed, the music had flowed through him.

But so did the anguish. He hardly ate or slept, guilt and regret plaguing him day and night. He wanted to run to her right now and beg for her forgiveness. But now was not the time. She had to focus on the Chamber Music Society's first performance of the season and the premiere of the new piece. Nevertheless, it took all his willpower to stop himself from running to her, and he didn't know how much longer he could last.

Meanwhile, he did everything he could to be worthy of her love. First was rewriting the string trio. What he'd written before had been good, but it wasn't the best that he could give her. She deserved his best. And this new piece was his love letter to her—his apology, his hope for a second chance. The music had begged to be written. Begged to be hers.

He'd also volunteered to conduct one of his own pieces with the chamber orchestra on opening night. The Chamber Music Society was so important to her, he wanted to help make their season a success. It had the added bonus of making him even busier than he was now. Rehearsals would take three to four hours out of his day until the performance two weeks from now. Maybe he would be so exhausted that he could sleep for a few hours at night.

Joshua desperately hoped he was doing enough to make Angie give him a chance to talk to her. All he wanted was a chance. Nothing he said might convince her to forgive him—fear struck through him at the thought—but he had to try. He had to show her that he trusted her and loved her with all his heart.

A glance at his watch told him that he needed to leave for his first rehearsal with the chamber orchestra. He hadn't conducted since his college days, but he knew what his music should sound like. He was confident that he would be able to work well with the orchestra. His only fear and hope was that he might run into Angie. All members of the Chamber Music Society were rehearsing at the performance center in preparation for the opening night.

He reread the email he'd been composing to Nexus before he hit send. Then he grabbed his suit jacket off the coat hanger and walked out of his office.

"Oh, good," Janice said. "You're leaving on time for once."

"I'm just stepping out for a few hours. I'll be back later this evening."

"You're going to burn yourself out working those outrageous hours," his assistant chided.

"I'm fine." He gave her a small smile. "I'll see you tomorrow."

Joshua made good time to the concert hall and walked in with excitement unfurling in his stomach. To hear his music played in front of him by a live orchestra, one that he was conducting, no less, would be exhilarating. It still amazed him how not having to hide his identity as A.S. anymore gave him so much freedom.

He stepped on stage with his heart beating hard in his chest. The dark wooden panels of the stage and the deep burgundy chairs filling the auditorium made everything all the more real to him. He'd stayed on the outskirts of the classical music industry for the past few years, and he was finally stepping into the middle of it.

The members of the chamber orchestra welcomed him with resounding applause. He bowed deeply at the waist, showing his appreciation, before taking the podium.

"I'm honored to be in front of this amazing orchestra." There was more applause. "It's beyond exciting to finally hear this piece played live the way I heard it in my head as I wrote it."

When he picked up the baton, the orchestra readied their instruments and gave him their full attention.

The music they made together filled him with awe

and humility. He never appreciated his decision to become a composer more than he did at that moment. And the darkness that had wrapped around him when he lost Angie lightened slightly. But his joy would only be complete if he was able to share moments like this with her.

When the rehearsal was over, he chatted with a few members of the orchestra out in the hallway, adrenaline still coursing through him. Then time stopped. Because when he looked up, he saw Angie standing a few steps away from him.

Her eyes widened in her pale face and she gasped. She'd lost weight and had dark circles under her eyes. He blamed himself for that. Even so, she looked so beautiful that heat prickled behind his lids. He wanted to run to her. Fall on his knees and beg for his forgiveness, but her sisters stepped protectively in front of her.

"Angie..." He took a step toward her.

"Mr. Shin," Megan cut him off. "Fancy meeting you here. Oh, wait. How could I forget? You're the famed composer A.S. I guess it isn't that much of a surprise."

Angie's gaze found his, then skittered away. Then her lips firmed into a determined line and she met his eyes again. She put a hand on her sister's arm and walked up to him. But she stopped just out of his reach. He clenched and unclenched his hands, forcing himself to stand still.

"Hello, Joshua." Angie's voice was distant but polite.

"Angie." He searched for something he could say

to her. Anything. "I hope the new string trio meets your approval."

"It's a beautiful piece. We're practicing hard to do it justice." She turned around to include her sisters in the statement.

"Speaking of practice—" Chloe stepped up and grabbed Angie's hand "—we should get going."

Without a backward look, the Han sisters walked past him into the concert hall. Steeling himself, he stumbled out to the parking lot and collapsed into his car. Seeing her only made him miss her more. The coldness in her eyes shot fear through him, but had he expected anything different? He had hurt her, but he would make it up to her.

They belonged together. He would prove it to her.

Fourteen

The first performance of the season always carried with it a special kind of anticipation that was felt by both the performers and the audience. It was a reunion after months apart. That anticipation was doubled this season because this was the first performance since the pandemic. The thrill of seeing each other was marred only by a certain nervousness about breaking the ice and getting comfortable with each other again after being apart for over a year and a half.

The Hana Trio was premiering Joshua's composition later in the program, and in the meantime Angie and her sisters stayed backstage, watching the chamber orchestra. The orchestra members were seated and ready, and their conductor took the podium. Slowly, the buzzing chatter of the audience quieted down, and anticipation built to a fever pitch in the ensuing silence.

As the first notes of the season resounded through the concert hall, chills ran down Angie's arms, a rare smile lifting the corners of her mouth. It happened every season, but the beauty of the music filled her with gratitude after the long absence.

Angie and her sisters erupted into applause along with the audience when the orchestra finished its first piece. Their fellow musicians had played beautifully and Angie was so proud of them. They worked hard and it showed.

She felt a tingling warmth on the back of her neck and knew that Joshua was standing behind her. He was there to conduct the next piece—his own composition. News of his special appearance had caused tonight's performance to sell out in record time. In a way, it was his debut in the music world. They had never seen him before.

It should feel incongruous that he was also the new CEO of Riddle Incorporated, but this version of him—both CEO and composer—was who he was meant to be. Despite her heartache, she was relieved to hear of his appointment as Riddle's CEO. She had been afraid that the revelation of his secret identity would give his rival an edge over him, but Joshua had done it. He would carry on his family's legacy just as he wanted.

But Angie still didn't know why he was going out of his way to help the society. He had to be busier than ever. Perhaps, it was his way of assuaging his guilt for breaking her heart. Well, that was his business.

Although she was trembling inside, she put a cool, professional expression and turned to face him.

"Joshua."

He looked unfairly handsome in his tuxedo, but she kept her gaze glued to his eyes.

"Angie," he said formally, and nodded at her sisters, who reluctantly acknowledged him.

When he made no move to walk past them, Angie figured he was nervous. They might not be lovers anymore, but they were fellow musicians. She wanted to help him. "Good luck out there."

Joshua's eyes widened in surprise, then a ghost of a smile appeared on his lips. "Thank you."

He finally walked past them, but looked over his shoulder at Angie for a long moment before taking the stage. Angie's heart stuttered at the longing in his eyes. No, she was just imagining things. There was nothing between them anymore. Even so, she walked closer to the curtains so she could watch him on the podium.

Silence fell over the audience again as Joshua lifted his baton. His movements weren't as practiced and artful as the conductor before him, but he moved with a natural grace and passion as he led the orchestra in his composition. She had heard this piece played many times over, but it sounded new and thrilling under his guidance. So this was how he heard the music in his head. Watching him conduct his own music felt like an intimate look into his soul. The audience was captivated, and she was with them. It was a performance she would never forget. When Joshua exited the stage through the other side, she pulled herself out of the trance.

"Girls, we're up," Angie said to her sisters. Pride filled her heart as she prepared to go out on stage.

She and her sisters were dressed in sapphire blue tonight. Angie wore a strapless, floor-length silk gown with an empire waist and a full, flowing skirt. Megan's asymmetrical one-shouldered dress hugged her figure and flared out midcalf like an inverted blossoming flower. Chloe had chosen a cap-sleeved, A-line dress with a sleek bodice. All the gowns were rich in color and simple in design. For a finishing touch, all three sisters wore identical black ribbons around their waists.

"We got this." Chloe shuffled her feet, wearing her game face, which was adorably incongruous with her formal gown.

"We're going to blow them away." Megan smiled with glowing confidence. "Let's go."

The three of them stepped out onto the stage. The auditorium was packed, and Angie's pulse quickened with adrenaline and anticipation. Playing live in front of such a big audience thrilled the performer in her. She and her sisters bowed to the applause and took their seats.

Vibrant silence descended in the auditorium once more and it was the Hana Trio's turn to fill the room with their music. Megan raised her bow, and Angie and Chloe followed suit. And at Megan's nod, everything fell away and the music took over.

Maybe it was her desire to do the music justice, or

maybe it was seeing Joshua bare his soul while conducting his piece, but overwhelming tides of emotion crashed into Angie and flowed through her fingers as she played. More than ever, she and her sisters played as one—as *hana*—and the sound they produced was stunningly harmonious.

When the final note played out, Angie and her sisters lowered their bows together. Thundering applause broke out and the audience jumped to their feet in a standing ovation. She and her sisters exchanged glances filled with awe and joy, and stood from their seats to take their bows. The applause continued even as they left the stage.

Still holding their instruments, they gave each other one-armed hugs, laughing and wiping away happy tears.

"I'm so proud of you," Angie said.

"I'm proud of us," Chloe chimed in.

"Me, too." Megan pulled their youngest sister to her and smacked a kiss on her cheek.

They put their instruments away and returned to listen to the rest of the program. The chamber orchestra played its final piece and the curtain closed. The backstage was soon awash with a sea of performers, conductors, directors and the society's board members. As colleague after colleague congratulated Angie and her sisters, she couldn't help but scan the crowd for a glimpse of Joshua. But he was nowhere to be seen.

What had he thought of their performance? Was he satisfied with the premiere of his new work? She hoped he was happy, and rightfully proud. If the audience's reaction was any indication, the piece was destined to be another success.

"Girls," Janet called out, walking across the room with her arms wide open. She pulled all of them into a group hug. "You sounded sublime. You made that string trio come alive."

"Thank you." Angie hugged her mentor back, glad to have made her proud.

Her sisters left to join the merry throng, and Janet continued, "I want to thank you for everything you did for the Chamber Music Society. Without your help, we would never have gotten A.S. to collaborate with us."

"You should thank him. I really didn't do anything," Angie said quietly.

She could hardly believe that it was only a few months ago that she barged into Joshua's office to coerce him into composing a new piece for the society. They had come so far from then, but now...it was all over. All her energy suddenly drained out of her.

"Angie, are you okay? You've gone pale," Janet said, holding her gently by the arm.

"I think I should call it a day. Everything turned out beautifully, but it's a lot," Angie said with a strained smile. "Can you let my sisters know that I left early to rest?"

"Of course, my dear." Her mentor studied her with worried eyes. "Drive safe."

Angie pulled her cello by her side as she walked to her car, hardly noticing her surroundings. She and Joshua had no reason to meet again. Everything they'd agreed to was wrapped up neatly with a bow. Searing pain dug into her chest and she could hardly breathe. It was really over.

When she got to her car, she hefted her cello into the rear and lowered herself into the driver's seat. She headed home, holding herself together. She wiped impatiently at the hot tears on her cheeks, struggling to keep her misty eyes trained on the road.

Would they still have been together if his identity hadn't been revealed? Maybe. She wouldn't have had the courage to leave him on her own. Then what? Would she have settled for their arrangement as long as she could be with him, even though it lacked true commitment? No. Their relationship would've ended sooner or later.

Being with him made her happier than she'd ever been. They had real affection and respect for one another. But that wouldn't have been enough. She deserved to be loved—wholeheartedly and without reserve. If he couldn't give that to her, it was better that it ended now rather than later.

Taking in a shuddering breath, Angie clenched her jaw to stop the tears from flowing. Her limbs felt leaden and she couldn't wait to get home. She just wanted to collapse into bed and sleep until she stopped hurting.

She drove past the front entrance of her apartment building to the attached parking garage, but screeched to a halt when she saw Joshua's tall form lit by the dim light of the entryway. Rolling down her window, she shouted across the street, "What are you doing here?"

"Can we talk?" he yelled back, running down the stairs toward her car. "I just want to talk."

Angie continued into the parking garage; she didn't want cars backing up behind her. What was he doing here? He wanted to talk? Talk about what? He was probably here to apologize for believing she could have revealed his identity. Should she give him that? Forgive him for not trusting her? Did she want to take that weight off his conscience?

She parked and walked down the corridor leading to the lobby and the main entrance. Joshua was leaning limply against the wall outside. His head and shoulders drooped low, as though they were too heavy for his body. Everything about his body language told her he was dejected…devastated.

Confused…and yes…worried, Angie rushed to open the door. "Joshua?"

His head shot up at the sound of her voice. At first, his expression was disbelieving, then something bright and vulnerable, like hope, lit in his eyes. "Angie. You drove away. I thought…"

She felt herself reacting to the light in his eyes, but shrank back in fear. She didn't want to feel hope for something that could never be. She wrapped her heart in another layer of armor. "Why are you here?"

He took a step closer to her and she flinched. The fragile hope in his expression seemed to dim a little, but he drew himself up and said in a determined voice, "I want us to talk."

"What's there to talk about? We've already said everything we could say to each other."

"That's not true. I… I have things left to say to you." His Adam's apple bobbed as he swallowed. "Things that have to be said."

What was the harm of one last talk? It broke her heart to see him, but never seeing him again was going to hurt more. If she let him in, she would at least be able to spend a little more time with him before they said goodbye forever.

"Fine. We can talk in my apartment." She stepped back and opened the door wider for him to come through.

They walked silently to the elevators, then down the gloomy hallway. Once they were inside her apartment, the space suddenly felt too small with Joshua's tall, broad body occupying it. Their formal attire seemed out of place in her cozy living room, but she sat down on the sofa and offered him the seat on the other end.

He sat and swiped his hand down his face. He looked haggard but still achingly handsome in his tux with his bow tie undone and hanging from his collar. Despite his insistence that they talk, he sat staring wordlessly across the room.

She wasn't impatient for him to start. Taking her time, she drank in every detail of his face and body. Being wrapped up in him had made her feel so safe and content. Would she ever find that with someone else? It seemed impossible now, but she had to hope that there would be happiness in the future for her.

"I'm sorry," he said, his voice breaking. "I'm so sorry, Angie."

"You're sorry?" Her voice rose as dormant anger

awoke in her. “So that’s why you wanted to talk. You want me to assuage your guilt.”

“That’s not true…” He reached out to her in entreaty but she evaded his touch.

“Isn’t it?” Tears prickled behind her eyes, but she refused to cry in front of him. “You thought I was the one who revealed your identity. And when I told you I loved you, you cast my words aside like you found it offensive. Now you want me to *absolve* you of that?”

“You deserve my apology a thousand times over but I don’t deserve your forgiveness. I hurt you and that’s something I have to live with. But please listen. All I want is a chance to explain…a chance to make it up to you.” His whole body stilled and his eyes seemed to will her to look at him. “I love you, Angie.”

“You don’t love me, Joshua.” Something between a sob and an incredulous laugh tore from her. “How can you love me when you believe I betrayed you? How can there be love without trust?”

“But I do trust you. And I know you’d never knowingly hurt me,” he said in a rush, as though he was afraid that he was running out of time. “I relived every moment of our horrible fight and forced myself to *feel* everything. I forced myself to face the truth. Angie, I never believed you betrayed me. Not even for a second.”

“Stop. Just stop.” She wanted to plug her ears and stop listening. The hope that filled her was so terrifying… If that hope shattered, she wouldn’t be able handle it. “You and I are finished. You made sure of that.”

Joshua knelt on the ground in front of her and

grasped her hand. She didn't pull it away, but she turned her head to the side.

"In the last few months, you showed me in so many ways that you loved me. You helped me get through my creative block with faith and patience, and you truly cared about my grandfather and played for him from your heart. Someone like that would never have revealed my secret to the world. You're incapable of doing something so selfish and calculating."

"None of that matters now." She jerked her hand out of his grasp and glared at him. "Your sudden change of heart only came after you found out who revealed your secret. You don't really trust me. Believing me now that you have concrete evidence of who betrayed you doesn't mean anything."

"I never believed you betrayed me. Please. My love for you isn't a *change of heart* and it has nothing to do with the bastard who exposed me," Joshua implored. "I only stayed away until now because I didn't know whether you would be able to forgive me. I didn't want to cause you more turmoil while you were preparing for tonight's concert."

"Trust goes both ways. Why should I trust you now?"

His eyes jumped around the room in a panic then light dawned on his face. "The new string trio. I wrote that for you before I found out who leaked my identity. I wrote that for you as soon as I realized I love you."

The tears she'd been holding back flowed down her cheeks. She was so confused. So lost. A vise gripped her heart and she couldn't take a full breath.

"Think, Angie. When did you receive the new piece from the Chamber Music Society? You got it before that bastard came to bask in the limelight, right?"

It was true. She received the new string trio just before the journalist came forward. Joshua had to have written it prior to then. But what does the new string trio prove?

"I was blocked because I was denying my love for you. How could I compose when I was lying to myself? I was able to compose the first string trio with your help, but it was still missing something because the lie held me back," he explained as though she'd spoken her question out loud. "Once I admitted to myself that I loved you, I knew I had to write you a new piece—one that was worthy of you. Unleashed from my lie, I was able to pour my everything into that music. That string trio is my apology, my love letter and my hope for our future. It is my soul. Surely, you felt that."

Angie covered her mouth as a sob broke through. She felt it all. She didn't allow herself to believe it, but the music had spoken to her. "If you love me, then why? Why did you push me away like that?"

"I was afraid. Fear held me back from admitting my love for you. Fear made me believe that you would inevitably leave me. I thought I could protect myself from more hurt if I pushed you away. I'm so sorry for letting you walk away believing that I didn't trust you. That I didn't love you." He grasped her arms and stared into her eyes. "I love you, Angie. More than life. Please give me a chance to make it up to you. I'll make you happy with everything in me."

She cried freely now, sobs wracking her body. He meant it. She felt it in her bones. He loved her.

"Please don't cry." He hesitated for a moment before he gently pulled her into his arms. "I can't take it. Please."

"I want to believe you." She wrapped her arms around his neck and hung on tight. He had found the courage to trust her with his heart again. Now she had to find the courage to accept his love. "No, I do believe you, but I'm so scared."

"I'm scared, too, but we can do this together. We're meant for each other. How else could I have fallen in love with the same woman twice?" He cradled her head with his hand. "I loved the girl you were and I love the woman you've become. You're the only one I've ever loved. Angie, you're it for me."

And he was the only one for her. She took a shuddering breath and leaned back to look into his eyes. "I love you, too. I never stopped loving you."

"Say it again," he whispered as though he might awaken from a dream. "Say you love me."

"I love you, Joshua." Her soul rejoiced at being able to freely say those words to him. Because he was hers. Hers to love. She cupped his beautiful face in her hand. "Tell me you're mine."

"I'm yours. Yours alone. Yours forever." His eyes roamed her face, filled with wonder and happiness. "I'm never letting you go again."

"Promise?" Her smile glowed from the depth of her.

"With all my heart." He smoothed her hair away from her face—his touch reverent. "I want to spend a life time with you if you'll have me. Will you marry me, Angie?"

"Yes." Her breath caught in her throat and tears filled her eyes again. The happiest tears. "I'll marry you."

Joshua cradled her face between his hands and kissed her with aching tenderness. She kissed him back with her heart singing, sealing their promise of forever.

* * * * *

If you love Angie and Joshua
don't miss the next Hana Trio story
by Jayci Lee,
coming December 2022 from
Harlequin Desire.

COMING NEXT MONTH FROM

HARLEQUIN

DESIRE

#2857 THE REBEL'S RETURN

Texas Cattleman's Club: Fathers and Sons • by Nadine Gonzalez

Eve Martin has one goal—find her nephew's father—and her unlikely ally is hotelier Rafael Wentworth, who's just returned to Texas and the family who abandoned him. Soon she's falling hard for the playboy in spite of their differences...and their secrets.

#2858 SECRETS OF A BAD REPUTATION

Dynasties: DNA Dilemma • by Joss Wood

Musician Griff O'Hare uses his bad-boy persona to keep others at bay. But when he's booked by straitlaced Kinga Ryder-White for her family's gala, he can't ignore their attraction. Yet as they fall for one another, everything around them falls apart...

#2859 HUSBAND IN NAME ONLY

Gambling Men • by Barbara Dunlop

Everyone believes ambitious Adeline Cambridge and rugged Alaskan politician Joe Breckenridge make a good match. So after one unexpected night and a baby on the way, their families push them into marriage. But will the convenient arrangement withstand the sparks and secrets between them?

#2860 EVER AFTER EXES

Titans of Tech • by Susannah Erwin

Dating app creator Will Taylor makes happily-ever-afters but remains a bachelor after his heart was broken by Finley Smythe. Reunited at a remote resort, they strike an uneasy truce after being stranded together. The attraction's still there even as their complicated past threatens everything...

#2861 ONE NIGHT CONSEQUENCE

Clashing Birthrights • by Yvonne Lindsay

As the widow of his best friend, Stevie Nickerson should be off-limits to CEO Fletcher Richmond, but there's a spark neither can ignore. When he learns she's pregnant, he insists on marriage, but Stevie relishes her independence. Can the two make it work?

#2862 THE WEDDING DARE

Destination Wedding • by Katherine Garbera

After learning a life-shattering secret, entrepreneur Logan Bisset finds solace in the arms of his ex, Quinn Murray. Meeting again at a Nantucket wedding, the heat's still there. But he might lose her again if he can't put the past behind him...

SPECIAL EXCERPT FROM

HARLEQUIN

DESIRE

Alaskan senator Jessup Outlaw needs an escape... and he finds just what he needs on his Napa Valley vacation: actress Paige Novak. What starts as a fling soon gets serious, but a familiar face from Paige's past may ruin everything...

Read on for a sneak peek of
What Happens on Vacation...
by New York Times *bestselling author Brenda Jackson.*

"Hey, aren't you going to join me?" Paige asked, pushing wet hair back from her face and treading water in the center of the pool. "Swimming is on my list of fun things. We might as well kick things off with a bang."

Bang? Why had she said that? Lust immediately took over his senses. Desire beyond madness consumed him. He was determined that by the time they parted ways at the end of the month their sexual needs, wants and desires would be fulfilled and under control.

Quickly removing his shirt, Jess's hands went to his zipper, inched it down and slid the pants, along with his briefs, down his legs. He knew Paige was watching him and he was glad that he was the man she wanted.

"Come here, Paige."

She smiled and shook her head. "If you want me, Jess, you have to come and get me." She then swam to the far end of the pool, away from him.

HDEXP0122B

Oh, so now she wanted to play hard to get? He had no problem going after her. Maybe now was a good time to tell her that not only had he been captain of his dog sled team, but he'd also been captain of his college swim team.

He glided through the water like an Olympic swimmer going after the gold, and it didn't take long to reach her. When she saw him getting close, she laughed and swam to the other side. Without missing a stroke or losing speed, he did a freestyle flip turn and reached out and caught her by the ankles. The capture was swift and the minute he touched her, more desire rammed through him to the point where water couldn't cool him down.

"I got you," he said, pulling her toward him and swimming with her in his arms to the edge of the pool.

When they reached the shallow end, he allowed her to stand, and the minute her feet touched the bottom she circled her arms around his neck. "No, Jess, I got you and I'm ready for you." Then she leaned in and took his mouth.

HDEXP0122B